After Dinner Conversation Themes
Research Ethics Edition
Philosophy | Ethics Short Story Fiction

After Dinner Conversation *Themes* – Research Ethics

This magazine publishes fictional stories that explore ethical and philosophical questions in an informal manner. The purpose of these stories is to generate thoughtful discussion in an open and easily accessible manner.

Names, characters, businesses, organizations, places, events, and incidents are either the product of the author's imagination or are used fictitiously. Any resemblance to actual persons, living or dead, events, or locales is entirely coincidental. The magazine is published monthly in print and electronic format.

ISBN 979-8-9896194-6-7 (Print)
ISBN 979-8-2244303-2-1 (Digital)
Library of Congress Control Number: 2023952704

https://www.afterdinnerconversation.com

After Dinner Conversation believes humanity is improved by ethics and morals grounded in philosophical truth and that philosophical truth is discovered through intentional reflection and respectful debate. In order to facilitate that process, we have created a growing series of short stories across genres, a monthly magazine, and two podcasts. These accessible examples of abstract ethical and philosophical ideas are intended to draw out deeper discussions with friends, family, and students.

Table Of Contents

* * *

From the Edition Editor

I made a prototype of a molecular sensor once. It was my graduate thesis project and took about two-and-a-half years. In the day-to-day tedium of baby-sitting reactions, serving as a teaching assistant, and managing my life outside of the lab, it never occurred to me to consider if this molecular sensor could be used for nefarious purposes or whether it had societal implications. It was just a molecular sensor. Why wouldn't that be a good idea?

Scientists were the children who asked incessant "why" questions, and, as grown-ups, decided to figure out the answers. Their ability to doggedly pursue a research question with single-minded focus is both the scientist's blessing and curse. By removing themselves from everyday distractions, they also remove themselves from the everyday implications of their experiments. It is the bioethicist's job to raise these questions, but like a doting new parent, researchers are prone to seeing all the good their research can do and none of the harm. That is where fiction comes in. Mary Wollstonecraft Shelley gave us an image of what it means to "play God" that is now part of our collective ethos even though the concept can be difficult to define.

In this collection of stories from After Dinner Conversation, we can imagine an abstract concept like Hana Arendt's banality of evil by meeting two men in a bar in "The Mind Reader," or the risks of dual-use technologies in "Cicada," and the problem of distributive justice and conflicts of interest in "Bugs in the Valley." "Mahabbah" asks whether scientists should tinker with human nature, while "Mayonnaise" is a story of unintended consequences. "We Don't Do Faux" and "Two-Percenters" have different takes on informed consent and whether one's privileged position is fair, while "Sow" considers ecological ethics and disrupting the natural evolution of a planet.

All these stories address research ethics questions, but rather than deliberating on things like utilitarianism and the greatest good for the greatest number of people, they show us a particular character in a specific time and place, so that we can ask ourselves, what would I have done in that situation?

Heather Zeiger – Editor

The Mind Reader

John Doble

* * *

It happened so long ago you'd think I'd just forget it. But I haven't, I can't; it's nested in my mind, coiled and twisted into my memory like a serpent I can't get rid of. I remember it at odd moments: when I'm eating breakfast or riding the train to work. Once I thought of it while I was making love. And each time I do, it remains as awful, as sinister and stunning as it was that night. But for reasons that keep changing. Different, elusive reasons I never fully understand.

It was the winter of 1973 and I was still in college. The country was at war in Southeast Asia, and in the summer, there were riots in the cities. Events that were deadly serious, yet with an unreality about them too. As if they weren't all they seemed to be, not something to take at face value. I remember anti-war protests that felt as serious as a rock concert: the air filled with music and the smell of marijuana, kids wearing red bandanas, waving Viet Cong flags, and chanting rhymes about how Ho Chi Minh and the National Liberation Front, the NLF, were going to win, like children sticking their tongues out or saying dirty words at dinner to see what reaction they could provoke. Even the young Black rioters interviewed on television seemed to pretend to feel angry when what they really felt was scorn, and perhaps a queer sort of pride that someone was paying attention. It was theater, a way of showing off. It wasn't real, not to the kids on campus, or the ones in the ghetto, maybe not even to those who told the police to shoot to kill. But of course, it was all real. And serious, deadly serious. I just didn't see it, didn't understand.

It was a Thursday night; we were in a college hangout called the Waystation, an old stucco building that had been there since the Revolution. Once it was a carriage house on the road from Philadelphia to Baltimore. The stage, then the train, would stop while passengers got out to stretch or eat a meal. I used to think about them, trying to imagine what they were like: gentlemen farmers, merchants, salesmen, immigrants, perhaps an occasional congressman who knew Henry Clay. No one knew who used to sit in that room, their boots drying in front of a fire, with a mug of ale and a trencher filled with stew. But now the place was run-down, seedy-looking; there was talk of tearing it down. The outside was cracked and peeling; hunks of stucco had been patched so often, they looked like tumorous sores. Inside, the great fireplace had been long ago bricked over and the planks on the floor were stained and worn, more gray than brown, with dust so thick you could move it with your shoe. People said it was owned by a speculator, that the university wanted the land for a new dormitory, and that only the price and some protestors from the historical society were holding things up. But students, being students, had made the place their own despite, or because of, the dirt and wear, the off-color draft beer, and the jukebox that played so loud it rattled your rib cage.

It was nearly nine o'clock, and I was at the bar. The room was crowded; it was always crowded on Thursdays. Students and former students and those who never were, mingled with a handful of faculty members, the younger ones, and a couple of "townies" looking for girls who believed in free love. They sat around cheap metal tables with red Formica tops, on chairs with rusted chrome legs and red plastic seats, laughing and talking and arguing about politics, philosophy, religion, and sex. And below the surface, beneath the loose talk and the laughter, lay a reality that few of them knew or cared about. I was like the rest of them. Jeffrey was not.

"People can be divided into two types?" Jeffrey was saying. "The weak and the strong?"

We were talking about psychology, my field of study, and a paper I was writing, and he was repeating what I'd told him about a personality test. The test had been developed after World War II by a group of psychologists who, shocked by what happened in Nazi Germany, had tried to understand how doctors and lawyers and bankers and businessmen—a population of law-abiding, God-fearing, ordinary people—could have taken part in it all, or at least stood there, watching it unfold, without trying to stop it, without crying out in protest. The philosopher Hannah Arendt coined the phrase the "banality of evil" to describe men like Adolph Eichmann who could be kind to children and animals, yet be part of a totalitarian machinery that murdered 12 million people: six million Jews from across the continent, and also homosexuals, gypsies, Russians, Ukrainians and other East Europeans;

civilians: old men, women, children. The psychologists had developed a test to discover what kind of person could do such things. In the psychology literature, it is called the "F-scale" the "F" standing for fascist. Elegant in its simplicity, the test consists of only five questions with which a person either agrees or disagrees. An extreme response, strong agreement or disagreement, on all five items, reveals, according to the test-makers, that a respondent has an authoritarian bent or fascist tendencies, and, inferentially, that he might well fall in behind someone like a Hitler or a Mussolini. Jeffrey had asked me what the five questions were and, when I'd told him, he latched onto one of them.

"People can be divided into the weak and the strong? Now I'm supposed to tell you whether I agree with that or not? And depending on my answer, you can tell if—what's the jargon you used—if I have an 'authoritarian personality?'"

It occurred to me later that I may have upset him, that what he did was a defense, a way of protecting himself from what he felt as an attack. But none of that occurred to me then. All I saw was that he was distorting what I'd told him, deliberately oversimplifying. I was sorry I'd brought the subject up.

"It's not *my* test," I explained again. "I didn't make it up. It's a standard test that has been used for decades. And that's only one of a series of questions. Someone has to answer *all* of them. Then, depending on *all* the answers, a psychologist can make a *guess*, an educated guess, about a *tendency* that *might* be part of someone's personality."

He smiled in that self-satisfied way of his, breathing deep and laughing once, so that his shoulder rose and fell. As if to suggest that life was so simple, so easy to understand, if only you saw it the way he did. But then, of course, the smile also suggested, that was too much to ask.

"How easily you dispense with human complexity," he said and then sighed affectedly. "Well, I do agree. Strongly." He seemed bored by the conversation. "Most people are weak, a few aren't. Now what? A psychologist—or a would-be psychologist— would say I'm what—a book-burner? That I want to exterminate people? Run a concentration camp?"

A TV was suspended above the bar, and someone had turned it on. I looked up and watched a powerful man in a red t-shirt and shorts slam an orange ball through an iron hoop. There was no cheering, no applause. The volume was turned down. It was the music, the loud, driving rock and roll music dominating all sound in the overcrowded room that caused the televised giant to run down the floor, waving a dark brown fist.

"Jeffrey, why are you ridiculing what I told you? Making it sound silly, like so much nonsense?"

I was trying to cut through his playacting, hoping that one question, one honest question, would change things between us. But he was like everything else around me: the jukebox, the furniture, the mirror behind the bar. Even if I had opened the door and let in enough air to clear out the haze and cigarette smoke, it would all still be there, it would all be the same.

"Is that what I was doing?" he said.

I felt anger build up inside me. He was patronizing me, treating me like a fool. Yet, naively, I persisted.

"Jeffrey, there are probably plenty of psychologists who might criticize that question, maybe the whole test. But their criticisms would be thoughtful, analytic. They wouldn't take it so... personally."

He signaled to the bartender that we wanted another round.

"Suppose I prove it?" he said. "Right here. Tonight. Suppose I prove that all your little textbook questions aren't worth the paper they're written on. If I did that, what would you think?"

As the bartender set two mugs of beer in front of us, I realized he aroused my curiosity. But instead of his question, I thought about him, about how well I knew him and what it was I knew.

Pale and thin, with dark curly hair, Jeffrey was not imposing to look at. A graduate student in photography, he was outstanding in his field, at least that's what people said. He'd had two shows and was already selling his work. He had few friends; I suppose I counted as one of them. But if not well-liked, he was always treated with a certain deference or respect. In part, I'm sure, because of his talent. But there was another reason too.

During that winter of protests and marches, it seemed as if he always wore his old army fatigues. And though he never talked about it, I had somehow learned what he'd done: He'd been a first lieutenant, won a Bronze Star and a Purple Heart. He led reconnaissance missions into Laos at a time when American troops weren't in Laos, at least according to the government. There was a day in the jungle when he surprised a North Vietnamese soldier and killed him with his bayonet. And an afternoon, years later, when—though I never heard him talk about the war, never criticize its wisdom or morality—he, along with a few hundred others, threw his medals over the White House fence.

His left hand was deformed, the tips of his thumb and forefinger missing. I'd heard it was caused by a land mine. It was gruesome looking, a reminder of a war I detested. But it was something else—a badge, a mark, something I secretly envied. For it was proof that Jeffrey had been tested. And come through.

In contrast, I was in my first year of graduate school. I was 23. My goal was to teach at a university. And though I never achieved it, I was, and am, generally content with my life. Except around Jeffrey. Then I'm aware of something else, a pinprick of a feeling, that I don't measure up, not to him. And that I never will.

"Prove it?" I said. "What do you mean you're going to prove it?"

"A demonstration." He waved his hand indicating the roomful of students. "With one of them."

He nodded toward the back. "See that girl? In the corner, in the sweatshirt. The one who looks like she's just been raped." He smiled coldly at the description. "Where do you think she's headed? A junkie, an alcoholic? Battered wife, unwed mother? All of the above? She's perfect, exactly what I need."

The girl sat at a table with two others. Above their heads, revolving slowly and illuminated from within, a half-dozen miniature horses, tan with shaggy white hooves, pulled a red beer wagon past green plastic trees. Around and around, they went, in circles, forever. Or until someone stopped them.

Her companions looked like they came from an earlier era. A pretty blonde in a tight-fitting sweater who looked like a cheerleader or sorority member was listening intently to a broad-shouldered fellow with short hair in a varsity jacket. But the girl with them, the one he'd singled out, was a child of the times.

Her eyes did not shine from too much beer; rather, they had a glazed, indifferent, faraway look signifying drugs or depression or both. Her sweatshirt looked slept-in, or as if she took it off at night, rolled into a ball, and put it under her pillow. Her hair, long and stringy and a dull shade of brown, hung down over her shoulders and full, unfettered breasts, sprawling onto the tabletop like so many roots from a dying plant.

I wondered what she had in common with the other two, why they were together in the first place. The girl seemed left out of the conversation next to her. As if she were there by accident or as a favor to someone. The blonde would lean back and laugh or reach across the table and take the fellow's hand. But the girl's expression, the dull, vacant stare, never changed.

I felt a kind of tired sympathy for the girl. She was like so many others, too many for one person to care about. In those days, it seemed like the campus was littered with kids just like her: who'd dropped out or run away, whose search for something they couldn't define led them to fill their bodies with drugs and live like vagabonds. Yet they were proud and defiant too, as if what they were doing was somehow true, or free, or spiritually authentic. I wished someone would turn off the music and turn up the volume of the basketball game.

"I need a strategy," Jeffrey said. "I can't just walk over and introduce myself. She'd have the advantage then, in spite of herself."

"What are you talking about?"

"You're a man of science," he said. "Think of it as an experiment. I'm about to conduct an experiment using that girl." His sigh was too heavy to be genuinely felt. "I wish there was someone who was more of a challenge, but in the interest of time..."

A look of concern must have crossed my face because, in a mocking tone, he said, "Don't worry, your liberal sensibilities won't be offended. I have no intention of harming her."

He was patronizing me again. I wanted to insult him and leave. Instead, I watched him reach for a piece of paper and on it, in large capital letters, print two words: "I KNOW." He showed me the paper, then folded it in half.

"We begin," he said.

Without glancing at her, he walked over to the jukebox near her table, dropped in a coin, and pushed some buttons. The girl did not notice him. Her expression, the dull, vacant stare, did not change.

On his way back and with seeming indifference, he bumped her chair and dropped the paper near her foot. She picked it up and waved it listlessly after him, then called out as he recrossed the room. But he paid no attention and rejoined me at the bar.

"You must not look at her," he said, and obediently, I turned away. "That was to get her attention. Now we wait."

It didn't take long. A moment later, she came up behind us and tapped him on the shoulder. But he did not respond.

"Hey," she said, tapping him again, "you dropped this."

Deliberately, he spun around on his stool, and when I turned too, I thought of his description: a girl who's just been raped. Her eyes were red, probably from marijuana. Her skin was blemished and sallow looking. And her clothes—a gray sweatshirt and a pair of faded jeans—hung on her like they belonged to someone else, as if she'd found them somewhere, tried them on, and decided to wear them anyway, even though they didn't fit. She couldn't have been more than twenty-one. But her tired, drawn, worn-out appearance made her look years older.

"You dropped this," she said, offering him the paper.

Jeffrey kept his hands folded in his lap, refusing to take it. In a tone that was nearly hostile, he said, simply, "I know."

The girl started. She stood there a moment, her outstretched hand holding her offering, and smiled tentatively.

"Is this a joke?" she said. "Some kind of joke?"

He ignored her question. "You read it," he said, and she colored slightly.

"It opened when I picked it up," she lied.

Jeffrey shook his head. "You had to read it." His tone was matter of fact. "You have no self-control."

The girl seemed to collect herself.

"Look, I don't know what's going on here but this is yours, right?" She waved the paper, and he nodded. "Well here," she flipped it into his lap, "if it's yours, take it."

She went back to her table, and Jeffrey stared at her. I was about to laugh at his "experiment" but he ignored me and stared at the girl.

She sat back down and pretended not to notice. But she knew he was watching. Self-consciously, she combed her hair with her fingers, then, after lighting a cigarette, made an attempt to join in her friends' conversation. All the time, Jeffrey stared. Finally, she crushed out her cigarette and stared back. Their eyes locked, and for a moment she glared at him, chin up, challenging him. Then her face relaxed, and she smiled, a tentative little half-smile, inviting him to respond. Instead, he spun around on his stool.

"Superstition," he said. "Signs, omens, magical thinking—that's what's important to her. She doesn't realize how important." He sipped his beer, and I thought of how a detective works, deductively, clue by clue, piecing things together. "She has no self-respect, anyone who looks like that... she probably hates her life, hates herself. But instead of doing anything about it, or trying to, she's waiting for someone to come along and do it for her. A stranger, a magician, some phantom from the back of her mind who'll ride in and whisk her up on his horse and carry her away to live happily ever after."

I thought about Samuel Beckett and his play, *Waiting for Godot*, and about the cults and movements and religious sects that had sprung up, and about the desperate kids who had run away to join them. I was about to mention all that to Jeffrey, but he continued to explain, and I did not interrupt.

"She's starting to wonder if I'm him, the one who's finally come. It's a simple enough dynamic. It happens all the time." He grinned, baring his teeth, and said, "Your crowd must have a name for it."

I don't know why I answered. I knew he was baiting me, treating me with the same contempt he felt for the girl. Yet for some reason, I felt the need to show I understood.

"A 'conversion experience,'" I said. "Someone who's predisposed to make a radical change. That's a term that comes to mind."

"Why *do* you people have to label the life out of things? 'Conversion experience.'" He nearly spit out the words. "When what you mean is pathetic little people leading pathetic little lives, hoping against hope that someone will come along and change it all for them. And someone will. Inevitably, they will find someone." He reached into his wallet for a ten-dollar bill. "But she's not quite ready so I'll help things along."

He handed the money to the bartender and ordered that a small glass of ice water be taken to her.

"She'll ask who sent it. The only thing you're to say is, she already knows." The bartender cheerfully agreed.

I watched in the mirror as he set the glass in front of her, said something, then shrugged. The girl looked up at Jeffrey. At his back.

At first, she ignored the water. Then she wrapped one hand around the glass and began tapping it lightly. She glanced our way, saw he still wasn't looking, raised the glass halfway to her mouth, leaned toward it and took a sip. She glanced up again and took another sip. Then she put the glass down and turned in her chair, as if making a final attempt to resist. Then, suddenly, as if overcome with a burning, unquenchable thirst, she grabbed the glass, lifted it to her mouth, and drained it, gulped it down. I told him what happened, and he nodded.

"A good choice, don't you think? Water? Necessary for life, yet so abundant, it's free. Of course it could have been anything—ashes, an animal, wine that represents blood. They're all incarnations of the same thing, aren't they? And so, the *form* doesn't really matter. It's the belief that's key. Of course, with her, I wanted the taking, the taking of something into her body."

What he said was chilling; it was so calculated, so piercing, so merciless. Yet fascinating too, darkly fascinating.

"She wants to believe now; she wants to believe in me." He motioned that we wanted another round. "But it's far from over. She'll probably come over. If she does, no matter what she says or asks you, you must not answer her. For me to do this without harming her, you cannot say a word."

He was being condescending again, and I got irritated. I sipped my beer and looked up. There was a commercial on the television, a time-out in the game, and I wondered what the score was. Before I could find out, the girl was standing behind us.

"Hey," she said, tugging his shoulder and spinning him around, "what's going on?"

He stared at her and did not reply, and she took her hand off him. "I said, what's going—"

"'What do you think?" he interrupted.

"I have no idea!" Her tone was indignant.

He reached around for his beer and took a long, slow sip. "I know," he said.

The girl took a half step backward. I could feel her unease.

"You drank the water," Jeffrey said.

"That was from you?"

The transparency of her ploy made him smile.

"Okay, so I knew it was from you. I was thirsty. So what?" He watched her, saying nothing.

"I said I was thirsty."

"I knew you were," he said.

The girl began to laugh, a nervous little laugh, more to herself than anything. As if to hear a familiar sound, to convince herself she was really here and this was really happening.

"This is creepy," she said. "This is really creepy. *You're* creepy and... Jesus, now you're gonna say 'I know' again."

The music seemed to blast louder than ever.

"Is this a game? Is this some kind of game?" she said.

"In a way," Jeffrey said.

"It is?" She was clearly surprised by his answer. Her shoulders hunched, and she began stroking her neck. One arm dropped straight down, her hand dangling; the other settled across her breasts. She seemed to muster something and her tone was flip.

"Suppose I don't want to play?" she said.

He shrugged, and she turned to go back to her table. She took a few steps in that direction, then changed her mind.

"You weren't going to stop me, were you? You'd just let me go back there. To them. *Them*." Her tone made it clear how she felt about her companions.

"Why would I stop you?" Jeffrey said. "Why would I want to?"

For the first time the girl looked at me. "What's going on here? What's this all about?"

But following his instructions, I did not reply.

She looked down, as if deciding what to do. The stool next to him was empty and suddenly, like a child in a drugstore, she bounced up on it and spun around.

"Okay, I'll play your game. What are the rules?" She laughed. "What are the rules? Does your game have any rules?"

"I don't want you to sit there," Jeffrey said.

She threw back her head and laughed, much too loudly to sound carefree as she wanted. "You think you're so cool. Who cares what you want? Who gives a flying fuck?"

He watched her for a moment, expressionless, then, without a hint of irritation, shifted on his stool, turning his back on her, dismissing her, shutting her out. His manner was totally controlled and icy cold.

The girl didn't know what to do. She sat there, gripping the chrome band of her stool with both hands, twisting herself back and forth like a child waiting to be told she was excused, that she could get up from the table and go out to play. Loudly, to provoke him, she said, "How'd you hurt your hand? Playing games with somebody else?"

He ignored her. Finally, when she realized he would continue doing so, she climbed down off the stool and came around to stand in front of him.

I thought of the way some parents discipline their children, giving or withholding love and approval, like a door that's open one moment, then slammed shut, until the child does what it's told. And when she obeyed him, when she'd climbed down and came around in front of him, he reopened the door.

"It happened in the war," he said. "Do you know what a land mine is?" The girl nodded. "We were on patrol, one of my men stepped on a land mine. He was blown apart. Like a firecracker. I was next to him."

I'm not sure why her manner changed so abruptly. In part, I'm sure, because of what he'd put her through: the way he'd humbled her, bent her to his will. And because his answer was so direct, so unexpected. But surely, too, because of what it was he said. We saw it on television every night, we marched, and we signed petitions. But few of us were really affected by that war. Not really. Not in the way he'd been. But whatever the reasons, once he answered her question, her whole demeanor changed.

"My God. I'm so sorry," she said. "I am so very, very..."

He shrugged. "The funny part is, it was one of ours."

"Oh my God," she said.

He sensed the change too, and in response, he became sympathetic, almost gentle. He shook his head, telling her without a word that it was all right.

"Things have happened to you too, haven't they?" he said softly.

The girl nodded, and her eyes filled with tears. It was as if, after all the back and forth, she had just decided to give in to him, trust him, to go along, no matter what that meant. She stood there, head bowed, like some disheveled prodigal ready to accept her penance.

"You've been through a lot, haven't you?"

"So much," she said. "So many things."

"And it's hard to explain, huh? Explain to anyone."

"Whenever I try..." She broke off, crying. She turned her head until she'd regained control. He gave her his handkerchief, and she wiped her eyes and nose. "Confusion, the confusion is terrible," she said. "About things they don't know *exist*."

"And tired? Tired of everything?"

"Sometimes," she began to tremble, "sometimes I think about..."

He reached out and stroked her cheek.

"Don't give in," he whispered. "You're closer to it than you think."

She nodded, smiled through her tears, looked up at him, and said, "I know, I'm going west—San Francisco. Actually, a little north, a town on the Russian River. The people there are so different, so laid-back and mellow..."

She was hoping for his approval, hoping he'd say that was just the thing to do—start again, turn the page, a new beginning.

Instead he wheeled and turned on her, snapped like a rattler, the door slamming shut.

"And that will change things?" His tone was insulting.

"It's different there," she pleaded. "People there have something going, something real, they're not so hung up..."

They were words she'd said many times. To herself and to others. But now, even before she finished, it was clear she no longer believed in them.

"It's over, isn't it?" he said. "Your daydream. Your last, best hope. You thought running away would change everything. You'd go to a magic place where things are different. Where *you'd* be different. Transformed. But I made you see it, didn't I? Made you see what a sorry little dream it is." He chuckled once, and his shoulders rose and fell. "Isn't it strange how things work out? I never saw you before tonight, and I've just changed your life."

"What's going on?" she said to me. "Please tell me what's going on."

Again I became aware of the music. Rock and roll, primitive, driving rhythms, so loud I could barely think. I began to answer, then felt his hand on my arm.

"What do you want to know?" he said.

"Your name," she said. "Tell me your name."

"My name's not important. But if you want to know, I'll tell you." He did. Then: "And yours?"

Hers was a frantic struggle now, an attempt to salvage something, a shred of self-respect from the ordeal she'd been through. "I thought you knew," she said. "I thought you knew everything."

Jeffrey smiled at her cruelly, one side of his upper lip

raised. "That's exactly what you thought," he said.

She staggered, as if punched in the chest. Then she said, "I know what you're doing—playing cat and mouse. And I'm the mouse."

He nodded.

"But *why*," she pleaded. "What in God's name do you want?"

"What do you think?"

She smiled knowingly and shifted her weight onto one foot, accenting her hip. She's attractive, I thought. In spite of herself, she's attractive. But his reaction was different than mine.

"Don't make me insult you," he said. She turned her head as if she'd been slapped. "Is that the only time you feel?" he said. "The only time you feel anything anymore? When you're high or getting laid? By someone? Anyone?"

It came pouring out now, the invective, as if he'd been restraining himself all along and could no longer hold back. "And when it's over, when you wake up in some strange bed or come down off your high, how do you feel? Disgusted with yourself? Empty? Used? Yet you keep doing it, don't you? Again and again. It's all you know anymore, isn't it? It's all that's left.

"That's why you came to me tonight," he continued. "Why you let me do it. Because whatever else I may be, I'm *real*. And with me, you are too. It's no exaggeration, is it? No exaggeration to say I make you feel *alive*! I woke you up from your stupor, your drugged-up daze. Humiliated you? Yes, I did... but you got something in return. Something precious, something you need—the feeling of being alive."

"Stop it," she said. "Please stop."

I'd had enough. I got up to leave, but she grabbed my arm

and looked at Jeffrey. "You can," she said to him. "You both can."

He grabbed her shoulder and shook her roughly. "Do you want to know what this is all about?" he said. She nodded, and again her eyes filled with tears.

"This was an experiment. You were the subject of an experiment."

"A what?" She couldn't believe what she'd heard.

He nodded at me. "We made a bet," he said.

"What kind of bet?"

"That I could manipulate you." His tone was casual, as if he'd just told her the time.

"To do what?" She began to cry. "I already said..." She rubbed her eyes with the back of her hands. "You have no right to do this."

"Why not? You enjoyed it. You enjoyed every moment."

"Maybe at first," she said.

"That's the first truthful thing out of your mouth," he said.

She nodded. Even in the midst of it all, she seemed pleased by his approbation. He continued. "We were having a discussion, an argument. In order to make my point, I had to find someone. I didn't have much time, so I needed someone easy, someone who's slovenly without any dignity or self-respect. I chose you."

She stood there, numb with disbelief.

"I didn't intend to puncture your balloon, end your little West Coast dream. That wasn't part of the plan. But now that I have," he softened his voice, "I want to make it up to you." He held out his hand, the mangled hand, stroked her hair and softly spoke her name. "Let me help you. Help you see what you've turned into. You still have time. It's not too late. I can help."

"How?" she sniveled.

"Go home and look in the mirror. Look at what you've let yourself become. Then do something about it. You can do it. I want you to. And when you have, come back. I'll be here. I'll wait for you."

"Go fuck yourself," she said. Her words were fiery, but her manner was meek and defeated. There was no fight left in her. She went back to her table. A moment later, she picked up her coat and left the room.

"Jeffrey..." I began.

"Not now," he said.

I lit a cigarette and looked up. Ten basketball players and two referees, out of sync with the music, were running back and forth, back and forth.

* * *

We waited almost two hours before she returned. In that whole time, we said nothing to each other. Not a word about what happened. I nursed my beers, careful not to get intoxicated, and waited.

If I hadn't been there to see her when she came back, I would not have believed it, the change was that remarkable. Instead of a runaway, or a pothead, she looked like a student. The sweatshirt had been replaced by a pale blue, oxford-cloth shirt with a button-down collar and a midnight-blue, V-neck sweater. Her jeans, though faded, looked neat and clean, and came down over the tops of a pair of polished black boots. Pulled straight back and hanging in a ponytail, her hair looked freshly brushed and seemed to shine in the haze of the room. Though she still wore no makeup except a trace of lipstick, her face looked smooth and her skin clearer. Even the dullness in her eyes was gone; they were alert and lively.

"Hello," she said, coming over.

Jeffrey smiled at her. "You look much better."

"I feel better," she said. "I wasn't sure you'd really wait. I mean, I know you said you would, but I wasn't sure." She took another step. "Can I sit with you? Wanna buy me a beer?"

He shook his head, and her body tightened. It was not the answer she'd expected.

"Why not?"

He reached out and caressed her cheek. "Because you don't need me to. Not anymore."

She stood there, letting him stroke her, then pressed her cheek against her shoulder, pinning his hand in place. He started to pull away, but she reached for his hand, held it in both of hers, then, softly, lay a kiss on the tip of his damaged forefinger, then his thumb.

"I understand," she said. "I think I finally understand."

"I think so too," he said.

She nodded and turned, and he threw some money on the bar. We were gone before she crossed the room.

As I started the car and pulled out of the parking lot, I told him he'd done a fine thing. He leaned back, his hands behind his head, and even in the dark I could see him smile.

"You still don't get it, do you?" he said.

I did not say a word.

"A fine thing," he said, sarcastically. "For Christ's sake, I could have done anything I wanted with that girl. *Anything*."

"But you didn't," I protested. "You could have, but you didn't."

"She'd have let both of us..."

"But you didn't," I said.

"*I* didn't, *I* didn't. But someone will. Others probably have. And others certainly will. She was easy for me, and she'll be just as easy for someone else... Maybe not tomorrow. But next week, next month..."

I drove in silence.

"But you," he said, half-turning in his seat, "you were worse. More difficult of course. But worse, so much worse."

I didn't know what he meant.

"With you it was intellect, intellectual curiosity. You watched. Damn it man, you *watched*."

He raised his voice. "How far would you have let me go? When would you have stopped me?

"'I'm not going to *harm* her, don't worry, it's all going to be fine.'

"I did it to her all right, but don't you see, I did it to you."

I watched him reach for a cigarette, his first of the night, and light it.

"Jeffrey," I said, "I want to tell you something. As a friend. Something you won't want to hear."

He stared straight ahead, and I said something I used to believe. "I think you're an angry person. Bitter. Maybe because of the hell you've been through. Jeffrey, I think you need help. There are people, professionals... I think you need to see someone."

He looked at me and smiled, and in that moment, I came to hate him. "I know," he said.

I turned on the radio and listened to two men analyze the results of the basketball game. I drove him home in silence, dropped him at his apartment, and did my best never to see him again.

* * *

This story first appeared in the After Dinner Conversation—September 2020 issue.

Discussion Questions

1. Do you believe, as the story mentions, that all people can be split into the weak and the strong? What does the story mean by "weak" and "strong?" Who in the story is weak and strong?
2. Do you believe that something like the F-scale can actually measure someone's preference for authoritarianism?
3. Do you think Jeffery (the person who talks to the woman) has the potential to be a "book burner," that is to say, an "authoritarian personality?" What aspects of his personality lead you to that conclusion?
4. Is having an "authoritarian personality" a good or bad thing? Why or why not? Is there something inherently bad to deferring to authority?
5. How is Jeffery's ability to manipulate the woman (and his friend) relevant to him proving the point he is trying to make? What do you think Jeffery has proven through his experiment? Is the narrator just as guilty because he watched it all happen and did *nothing*?

* * *

Mahabbah

Logan Thrasher Collins

* * *

"I know this might sound kind of wild, but I've got a plan to save the world," Jacqueline said to Aziz, gazing at him with her vivid blue eyes. They were out to lunch at Al Jyr, sitting beside a window. Their table sported a vase filled with azure hyacinths and the window overlooked a dusty street several floors below. "You see, I made a new type of virus that... well, it changes people for the better." Jacqueline continued, "The virus edits a few genes, rewires some neurons, and changes the levels of some hormones. It turns us humans from nasty tribalists into far more compassionate people."

"You're kidding." Aziz smiled.

"No, really!" Jacqueline insisted. "There's been a lot of hatred, cruelty, and pain all over the world. I think this virus is gonna fix things. I call it Mahabbah and its name means love."

"Okay... really?" Aziz's playful smile faded. "I mean, really?"

"Yes. I built a virus in the lab that increases people's

empathy. I've tested it on the monkeys. Had to pretend that I was doing something else to keep folks from finding out though. That's the other thing... I'm planning on releasing Mahabbah myself. You know how conservative people are about this stuff. I mean, I realize Fakhoury is a lot better about women's rights and freedom of religion and all that than the rest of the Middle East and even the rest of the world for that matter. But still, something as radical as Mahabbah would never get off the ground if I told people about it."

"So why are you telling me?" Aziz asked, sitting back in his chair and trying to absorb what he was hearing. "I mean... aren't you worried I'll report you?"

"Well, I feel like I can trust you." Aziz thought about it for a few moments. He looked at Jacqueline and felt a rush of warmth. He had known her since his first year as a graduate student at Fakhoury University. He recalled a time when they had sat on the edge of a fountain after their seminars had finished. Jacqueline had taken off her shoes and swung her feet into the water. She had invited him to do the same. He had protested at first, but her bright enthusiasm had soon induced him to laugh and follow suit.

"Okay, so you can trust me," he admitted. "But I do have some questions. First of all, if you've only tested it on marmosets, how do you know it's safe for humans?"

"I thought you might say that. I've got a version that can't spread between people... and I have actually tested it on one human being. I infected myself two weeks ago."

"Oh my gosh, are you... are you okay?"

"So far so good," Jacqueline told him. "I've been performing a variety of medical tests on myself. The virus seems safe to use on humans. That said, even though a whole series of clinical trials isn't really practical if we want to keep this a secret, I want to have at least one more test subject." Aziz pondered her words for a moment as he looked out the window at the ornately painted building across the street.

"I suppose you want me to be the next test subject?" he asked. Jacqueline nodded.

"I'll need some time to think about it of course," Aziz told her.

"Of course." Jacqueline smiled wryly. "It's a big decision."

The next day, Aziz had difficulty focusing on the morning lecture in his Middle Eastern literature seminar at Fakhoury University. He stared straight through the professor, a middle-aged man with a thick black beard, not hearing the words of the lecture. Light from the hot desert sun outside poured through a row of windows at one side of the room, causing the classroom to get uncomfortably warm.

Aziz thought about Jaqueline's plan, wondering if he was crazy to consider going along with it. He had seen Jacqueline demonstrate brilliance many times, not just in engineering, but also in her capacity for kindness. He recalled one time during the previous summer that Jacqueline had given an entire box of leftover pastitsio to a homeless man after they had eaten lunch.

"Are you listening Aziz? We are discussing the tragic romance of Layla and Majnun," the professor asked.

"Oh, sorry. I'll make sure to pay attention. Sorry," Aziz responded quickly. The professor sighed but did not chastise Aziz further.

Aziz met Jacqueline that afternoon at her apartment. She lived on the fourth floor of a white stucco building decorated by a mural of interwoven blue and yellow flowers. Her quarters were small yet comfortable, with a window overlooking the rest of her neighborhood. Palm trees swayed in the breeze and the pale dome of a small mosque was visible underneath the evening sky.

"So, I've got a dose of Mahabbah in here, the one that doesn't spread between people," she said as she opened her refrigerator and pulled out a small silvery aerosolizer. "Have you decided if you want to do this?" she asked more quietly.

"Yeah... I'm gonna do it. I think that the world needs this and if anyone can pull it off, you can. It all just seems a little crazy, y'know?" Jacqueline nodded and then hugged him tightly.

"I know," she whispered. "Honestly, I've been struggling with it myself. But I just can't let the world keep going the way it is. Just today, I heard about some more supremacist bombings of churches in the United States." She held up the aerosolizer. "I put it in here. When you inhale it, the virus will travel through your olfactory receptor neurons and go to your brain." Aziz took the aerosolizer from her and positioned it under his nose. He glanced at Jacqueline. In the dim light of the apartment, her blue eyes seemed to glitter as if full of stars. Aziz pressed the button on the aerosolizer and inhaled deeply, feeling the tingly sweetness of the device's contents as they entered his nostrils. He lowered the aerosolizer and grinned weakly.

The next morning, Aziz thought about Mahabbah as he walked to Fakhoury University. He knew that Jacqueline's plan held certain risks. The virus might exert unforeseen side effects in some people. Her plan also involved altering the personalities of eight billion people without their consent. Aziz knew that unilateral action, even when motivated by the greater good, had a dark history. Yet he could not help himself but to trust Jacqueline. Her dedication to compassion and her vision for a future full of hope were intoxicating. Aziz could see Fakhoury's skyscrapers across an artificial lake. Among them, Burj Muntasaf Allayl stood more than twice as tall as the next highest building in the city. Even though its walls were as black as obsidian, Burj Muntasaf Allayl blazed under the morning sunlight as if it were lit by a divine flame. Aziz closed his lids and took a deep breath. He thought of Jacqueline's glittering blue eyes. He believed in Jacqueline. He could not turn back.

A few days later, Aziz was walking through a courtyard on the Fakhoury University campus when he saw a young woman crying on a bench. He felt a surge of sadness and an intense desire to take care of the young woman. She wore a white hijab and a coat with gold buttons. She was trembling slightly as she wept with her head in her hands. When Aziz arrived, the young woman looked up with embarrassment.

"I'm sorry. I'm sorry," she said. "I... my sister... she's gone." Aziz sat down next to her.

"It's okay. I hope that I'm not disturbing you. I just want to help," he said. "I know that there's probably not a lot I can do. But I just want you to know that I'm here if you need me. It's okay to feel whatever you need to feel. Is it alright if I put my arm around you? I won't be offended if you say no. Even though things have changed a lot in Fakhoury, I know there're still some people who have religious reasons to not want to be touched."

"It's okay," the young woman said tearfully. So, Aziz placed his arm over her shoulder. She continued to sniffle, but he could feel her trembling grow less violent. After a few minutes, she looked up at him gratefully.

"What's your name?" she asked.

"I'm Aziz. What about yours?"

"My name is Dina," she replied. "My sister Mounira... she committed suicide. I should have known... I should have done something..."

"It's not your fault," Aziz told her, trying to make his voice sound both firm and tender. "I've had a few friends who've had someone close to them... and they all worry about that. But believe me, you are not to blame. I realize that might be difficult to see right now and that's okay. But I think that you will come to know in time that it's not your fault."

"Thank you," Dina told him. "I can't tell you how much I appreciate your help." After that, Aziz walked Dina to the mental health center on campus and gave her his phone number in case she needed to talk to him again. It was only after he had sent her inside that Aziz realized that he was more than thirty minutes late to his Greek poetry seminar.

That evening, Jacqueline called Aziz on the phone and asked him to meet her back at her apartment to check his physiological condition. As he walked to her neighborhood, the sun was setting, casting a tangerine glow over the palm trees and the rooftops. By the time he arrived at Jacqueline's building, a spray of glittering stars had started to bleed through the dying light of the sun.

When Aziz arrived at Jacqueline's apartment, he found her crying softly. He rushed over and sat down on the bed next to her, putting his arm around her instinctively. He did not speak, instead allowing her to bury her head in his shoulder until she was ready to talk. After a minute or so, Jacqueline raised her face and looked up at Aziz.

"I'm sorry Aziz." Jacqueline sniffled. "I'm just feeling overwhelmed. There're all these people all over the world who aren't nearly as lucky as we are. They're losing their loved ones and struggling to survive and starving to death and being murdered. Life on Earth is just one big mess of pain and grief. It's all so awful, I can hardly stand it." Aziz pulled her close again.

"I know," he replied. "But you're doing something about it. Mahabbah might not fix everything, but if everyone felt the way you do... things would get a lot better. I mean, it has already helped me to do some good. Earlier today, I helped comfort a girl who lost her sister. I don't think I could've done that properly if not for Mahabbah."

"Are you sure this is gonna work out?" Jacqueline said. "I mean, look at me. I'm a mess. If everyone gets infected with this... I mean, I don't want to hurt people. I want to help them. I don't want everyone to be so damn sensitive that they can't function."

"Well, how often have you felt like this?" Aziz asked.

"It hasn't been this bad until now," Jacqueline admitted. "But I'm still worried."

"I think you're gonna be okay, but I'll be right here with you whatever happens," he told her. Jacqueline took a few deep breaths.

"You know what? I think we should explore the city tonight," she said suddenly. "Take a little break from talking about Mahabbah and go on an adventure."

So, Aziz and Jacqueline went down to the parking lot and called a car. After a short drive, the car dropped them off in the downtown part of Fakhoury. Rows of skyscrapers towered into the air, their windows blazing in a great tapestry of yellow and white lights. The crescent moon shone down upon the city while the stars spread across the night like an ocean filled with tiny phosphorescent jellyfish.

"C'mon," Jacqueline said, tugging on Aziz's arm. She wore a blue bow in her raven hair and Aziz thought that she looked quite beautiful. Back when they had first met, Aziz had entertained the possibility of a romantic relationship with Jacqueline, though he had long since decided that she probably did not think of him in that way. But tonight, under the glittering illumination of the city and the stars, Aziz wondered if perhaps some spark of romance could emerge after all.

Jacqueline took him to Zahr Fakhoury, a park filled with luxurious gardens. Marigolds and purple hyacinths were braided across archways. Pale pink rose bushes bloomed alongside shocking blue lilies. As Amir and Jacqueline walked through the gardens, they came across a series of circular pools that were illuminated from beneath the water. Scarlet lotuses swam on the surfaces of the pools, their petals lit from below. Jacqueline took Aziz's hand in hers for just a few seconds as they marveled at the pools before letting go. She then stepped forward and stroked the lurid petals of a lotus near the edge of one of the pools.

After exploring the garden, they visited Burj Muntasaf Allayl. The skyscraper stood at the center of a plaza which was made entirely from black marble. Glowing fountains lined the walkway up to the entrance. Aziz looked up at the building as he and Jacqueline approached. Though its walls were mostly sided with the same black marble as in the plaza, light shone out of its tens of thousands of windows all the way to its distant summit. Burj Muntasaf Allayl stood over a kilometer in height. From this vantage point, Aziz thought that the Burj Muntasaf Allayl seemed so tall that it could have been built by gods or some advanced alien civilization rather than humans. Once inside, he and Jacqueline took an elevator to the observation deck on the ninety-eighth floor and looked out upon the gleaming expanse of Fakhoury.

"It's so beautiful," Jacqueline whispered as she gazed across the city's vast tapestry of light. Above the city, the crescent moon was visible in the star-filled sky. Jacqueline turned to look at Aziz, her eyes sparkling with wonder. "Thanks for helping me out tonight," she said softly. Aziz put his arm around Jacqueline as they continued to look over the city.

Later, Aziz was in good spirits as he walked Jacqueline back to the apartment building. When they said goodnight, Jacqueline looked into Aziz's eyes. He felt a little dizzy as he gazed back at her. Jacqueline quickly kissed him on the cheek before her own cheeks turned pink and she hurried upstairs.

The next day, Aziz called Jacqueline after his seminars were over, but her phone went to voicemail. He tried again an hour later, yet still received no answer. So, Aziz went to the lab where Jacqueline had been working since her second year of graduate study. He walked briskly up to the Fakhoury University Biomolecular Engineering Center. In the parking lot, he saw a group of sleek white police vehicles as well as several glossy black armored trucks. His heartbeat quickened and he felt a surge of fear. When Aziz approached the front door of the building, a man in a beige camouflage uniform stepped out in front of him. The man wore dark glasses and carried a machine gun at his side.

"You can't enter. Building is closed off. Biohazard," the

man stated flatly.

"Do you know what happened?"

"Can't talk about it."

"I have a friend who might have been in there, is there anyone I can talk to who might be able to help me find her?"

"No. You have to leave this area now." Aziz stepped back and looked up at the fourth floor of the structure, trying futilely to see through the windows of Jacqueline's lab. But when the officer placed his hand on his gun, Aziz scurried away. He felt lightheaded with terror as he jogged towards the campus's main office, hoping to discover more information. On his way, he heard a familiar voice.

"Hey Aziz! Are you alright?" Dina called. Aziz stopped, breathing heavily.

"Sorry... I'm not sure... do you know Jacqueline? She works in the biomolecular engineering building. There're a bunch of armed men over there."

"Oh my gosh! But yeah, I think I know who you're talking about. Do you mean Jacqueline Faucheux?" Aziz nodded rapidly.

"Yeah. Jacqueline's a close friend of mine. I couldn't get ahold of her by phone and when I went to check her lab, a guy with a machine gun told me to leave because of a biohazard."

"Oh no! That's awful. I really hope she's okay," Dina exclaimed.

"I think I know what happened," Aziz blurted.

"What do you think is going on?"

"Well... never mind," Aziz said quickly. "Sorry. I don't know if I can say."

"You can trust me. I owe you one for helping me out

yesterday. Besides, I like Jacqueline. She's a nice person. I promise you that I won't do anything that would cause her harm." Aziz thought for a few seconds before replying. He did not wish to reveal Jacqueline's secret, but he decided that these dire circumstances required drastic action.

"Jacqueline built a virus that she calls Mahabbah... but it does something good rather than causing a disease. It gives people more empathy. She did this without telling anyone except for me. She's tested a non-contagious version on herself... and on me."

"Wow. Okay." Dina marveled. "So, I guess that's how you knew exactly what to say yesterday when... well you know." Aziz nodded weakly. "You think that these military people are here because of the Mahabbah virus?"

"Yes. I'm just terrified that they're going to hurt her or lock her up forever or something!" Aziz's words tumbled out. It was then that he felt his phone buzz in his pocket. He pulled it out, hands trembling before putting the phone to his ear.

"Jacqueline! Are you okay?" he asked.

"Well sort of... I'm stuck inside the biomolecular engineering building, hiding in a closet. Sorry I couldn't talk sooner, there were soldiers in the hall, searching the building." She took a deep breath. "I'm going to ask you for a favor that might get you in big trouble. I want you to go to my apartment and look in my refrigerator. You'll find a pink shoebox. Inside is an aerosol can. I need you to take it to the Fakhoury airport and spray it all over. Pretend that it's air freshener or hairspray or something. I made this version of Mahabbah infectious enough that it should spread all over the world from there." She paused. "If we don't meet again, I just wanted to say that I love you. Oh no, I've gotta go now, I hear people coming." Jacqueline hung up. Aziz quickly explained to Dina what Jacqueline had asked of him.

"I want to do it," Aziz confessed. "But I can't just leave her behind."

"I know there're probably a bunch of bioethical issues with this whole thing. But I think that you need to do this," Dina told him firmly. "If you don't, they might find out and stop Mahabbah from ever getting out there. There'll never be another chance for it. I'll watch the building and try to help Jacqueline in the meantime." Aziz looked back at Dina, knowing that he probably looked terrified out of his wits. Yet when he had spoken to Dina the day before, he had seen Mahabbah's power for good. He loved Jacqueline as well. He knew that she needed him to take this action.

"Please just make sure she'll be okay," he told Dina before dashing away and hailing a self-driving car to take him back to Jacqueline's apartment. While Aziz rode in the vehicle, his thoughts raced. He wondered if he was doing the right thing by releasing Mahabbah into the world. People would have no choice but to have their very souls altered by the virus. As he looked out of the car's window, he saw Burj Muntasaf Allayl on the skyline, gleaming darkly in the afternoon light.

Aziz felt as though he was in a trance when he stepped out of the car and set foot in Jacqueline's familiar neighborhood. He passed the dome of the small mosque and the gently dancing palm trees. He could sense a sort of electricity flowing through his body. He was about to do something that could alter the trajectory of human civilization forever. He climbed the steps to Jacqueline's apartment, passing a series of potted blue hyacinths in the stairwell. He thought of all the horrors endured in human history. He shivered with sorrow as he heard the screams of pain and terror and the panicked voices of the downtrodden. Humans were capable of hurting and hating and killing. But humans also held the seed of goodness inside of themselves. He could see Jacqueline's vision, her desperation to raise that seed into a blossom of kindness, a flower that would spread across the Earth and transform humanity for the better. Despite his doubts, Aziz believed in this vision.

He went into Jacqueline's apartment and retrieved the pink shoebox from her refrigerator. Aziz carried the box down to the street and called another car, this time instructing the vehicle to carry him to the Fakhoury International Airport. He was dropped off at a baggage check area. The great white wing of an overhang swept along the shining glass side of the building. The bustle and smoke of traffic seemed to blur as Aziz walked into the airport and pulled the aerosolizer out of the box. Aziz took a deep breath, looking around the crowded airport lobby. Crowds of people were lined up to check their luggage.

Aziz raised the slim golden aerosolizer and pressed the button to release Mahabbah. The stream of mist bloomed into a cloud before dissipating. Aziz walked briskly to another spot and pressed the button again, looking around anxiously to make sure he was not arousing any suspicion of illicit activity. He continued until the can was empty of its contents. At last, he tossed the can into a bin and hurried out of the airport, calling another car to take him back to Fakhoury University.

When he returned to the biomolecular engineering building, he saw several white vans emblazoned with scarlet biohazard symbols alongside the military and police vehicles.

Officers with machine guns were still milling around the area. Aziz could see a few men in hazmat suits as well. He spotted Dina and rushed over.

"Did you do it?" Dina asked.

"I did," Aziz replied, not quite believing his own words as he thought back to his actions in the airport. "Have you seen Jacqueline?"

"No, but I did find something out. I ran into someone who worked in the biomolecular engineering building. He said that a technician in one of the primate labs had seen weird hormonal changes in some of the monkeys. He found an unidentified virus in some blood samples and reported it." Aziz cursed under his breath before looking over to the horizon and sighing with worry. The orange disk of the sun had started descending and long shadows populated the campus. Reddish illumination reflected from the parked vehicles around the biomolecular engineering building. That was when Aziz spotted a pair of men in hazmat suits leading Jacqueline out through the front doors of the building.

"Jacqueline!" he cried out, starting towards her. But another man in military gear stepped in front of him.

"Quarantine. You have to stay away," the man snarled. Jacqueline looked over to Aziz helplessly as she was led into one of the biohazard vans. Aziz saw her enter the vehicle, heard the engine rev, and watched the van drive away. Dina put a hand on his shoulder as a tear rolled down his cheek.

Later that night, Aziz lay in bed, watching the blades of his ceiling fan swish through the warm air. He felt his phone vibrate. Though the phone said that it was an unknown caller, he picked up anyways. His heart leapt when he heard

Jacqueline's voice.

"Hi Aziz."

"Oh gosh, are you okay?" Aziz asked urgently.

"I'm fine. They put me in a government hospital, but no one has hurt me. I might be stuck here for a while though... and I heard that they searched my apartment." Aziz could tell that she was scared that the officers might have found the box if he had not removed it from the refrigerator.

"I did what you asked me to do," he said to her. "Left it at the airport after."

"Good. Thank you." She sighed with relief. Aziz was relieved as well. He did not want to think about what might have happened to her if the officers had found the box. After he spoke to Jacqueline, Aziz texted Dina to let her know that Jacqueline was alright.

"Oh, I'm so glad!!" Dina responded.

It was nearly two months before Jacqueline was released from the hospital. In that time, Aziz began to hear of the spread of a mysterious virus across the globe. According to Al Jazeera, neuroimaging had shown that the virus was causing changes to the human brain. Though these changes were not yet fully understood, the virus seemed not to result in any major ill effects. On the contrary, people reported experiencing feelings of goodwill and surges of almost superhuman capacity to help others through their troubles. Some people began to claim that the virus was a gift from Allah, seeded on Earth to restore peace to humankind. Though this supposed divine origin was controversial, peace did begin to gain traction.

Treaties quickly resolved some brutal skirmishes in Cambodia. Rates of violent crime in the United States plummeted. Numerous European politicians made sweeping changes to their platforms, taking direct action to help protect the downtrodden. The world saw a tremendous rise in charity. Even the extremely wealthy began to redirect the efforts of their corporate empires towards humanitarian applications such as treating diseases and cleaning up pollution. Systems were implemented to ensure that surplus food and medicine could be more easily transported to people in need. After a decade of people grimly prophesying that humanity was on the path to ruin, the flame of hope had returned to civilization.

Aziz spent some more time getting to know Dina and continuing to help her through the loss of Mounira. They hung out at coffee shops, drank chai, and ate baklava. He learned that she was studying chemistry and that she played the viola. He found out that Mounira had been musically talented as well and that she had performed a cello concerto at the Fakhoury Opera House when she was just seventeen years old.

"I wish that Mounira could have lived to see the new world that Mahabbah is creating," Dina told Aziz, tears in her eyes. Aziz put his hand on Dina's.

"I know that she loved you very much, so even though she's gone, I think that she would be happy to know that this is the world in which you're living."

As soon as Jacqueline came out of quarantine, she and Aziz met back at Al Jyr. They embraced joyfully outside of the restaurant. Jacqueline ran up to Aziz and threw her arms around him. She kissed him on the lips as he picked her up and spun her around. After that, they went inside the building, chatting away happily.

* * *

This story first appeared in the After Dinner Conversation—August 2021 issue.

Discussion Questions

1. Can humanity be "made better," or is it already perfect? Are there biological reasons why humanity may need the traits that we consider undesirable?
2. According to the story, the world would be better if everyone had more empathy. What other traits, if any, should humanity have that would make the world better?
3. Is there a difference between prescriptions for individuals to improve human qualities, and a general prescription that improves all of humanity as in the story?
4. If you were in the position to release the drug, would you have released it? Is there a difference between changing the traits of people *(as in the story)* and simply removing the means for people to act on those traits *(the tools of violence)*?
5. Are the people in the story now better people or does being a better person require the freedom to make better choices?

* * *

Mayonnaise

Viggy Parr Hampton

* * *

You know what they say: when life gives you ASS, you make mayonnaise with it. That's exactly what Dr. Loriah Harp and the good folks at Natural Light Foods did. And they didn't hide the ASS at the bottom of a label, either—their entire marketing campaign championed its use. Natural Light Mayonnaise: The Condiment with sASS!

Or, on some posters in gentrifying or otherwise chi-chi neighborhoods: The Condiment with clASS!

Commercials trumpeted the unmatched greatness of Natural Light Mayonnaise with loud colors and even louder shouts of "Zero percent fat! Zero percent calories! One hundred percent flavor!"

And...the public bought it, wholeheartedly. I'm sure you bought it, too. They bought into the marketing, they bought into the promises, and, most importantly, they bought the product. They smothered their turkey sandwiches with Natural Light Mayo, they drowned their potato salads, they scrambled it into their eggs, they even baked it into their cakes and cookies. Restaurants advertised it proudly on their menus: "We only use Natural Light Mayonnaise!"

Natural Light Mayo had the Midas touch: everything it smothered, covered, or stuffed turned into a health food in the eyes of the customers who bought it by the barrel. And Dr. Loriah Harp and Natural Light Foods made, in short, a ton of money over the next six months.

* * *

Loriah, an employee at Natural Light Foods, and the inventor of acetylsterolstearate (ASS), which made Natural Light Mayonnaise possible, was nothing if not anti-hypocritical. That is to say, she practiced what she preached. She drank the Natural Light Mayo Kool-Aid (not a real product yet but hey, it was only a matter of time) and made sure to keep her own fridge stocked. Then there was the true test of her loyalty: she fed Natural Light Mayo to her family. Liberally.

"Mom, what's for dinner tonight?"

Loriah paused, realizing that she was about to lift a spoonful of Natural Light Mayo straight from the jar to her lips, completely missing the upturned slice of bread on the counter. She laughed, embarrassed, and spooned the mayo onto the bread. She turned to face Alex and smiled. "Tonight's menu features turkey and cheese sandwiches and baked french fries with a side of the amazing, the delicious, the healthy...Natural Light Mayo!" Perhaps Loriah was a bit of a showman as well.

Alex grinned. "You know, even though we've had mayo at pretty much every meal, I'm still not tired of it."

"Me neither, sweetie. It really is a miracle product."

Clint walked into the kitchen and kissed Loriah on the

cheek. "I hope we're getting more of that delicious mayo tonight!" His new Gucci slippers squeaked on the wood floor. He checked his new Rolex and announced, "It's nearly time for Family Game Night!"

"After a healthy dinner, of course!" Loriah said.

"Of course," Clint answered, beaming.

"I'll go set everything up," Alex said, walking off into the dining room.

* * *

You're probably thinking this family portrait is a dead ringer for Norman Rockwell, huh?

* * *

Alex collapsed halfway through their second game of Trouble. First, his eyelids started to twitch and flutter, then a thin river of blood trickled from one nostril, followed by a loud sneeze that sprayed blood all over the table and the pallid faces of his horrified parents. His head slammed down onto the game board, sending yellow, blue, and red peg pieces flying like shrapnel through the air.

He convulsed a few times, his forehead pressing the plastic bubble once, twice, three times, the die inside popping wildly like popcorn. Finally, his exhausted body stilled, and the blood from his nose pooled and congealed on the game board.

Loriah looked at Clint and Clint looked at Loriah, both too astonished to speak. After what felt like an interminable silence, Loriah coughed and said, "Clint. I think we need to take Alex to the emergency room."

* * *

Loriah watched her son with cautious optimism as he spooned hospital potato salad (made with Natural Light Mayo, of course) into his mouth. He paused to slurp orange juice through a silly straw, the sucking noise sounding like a grenade blast in the quiet room.

After his 'episode,' as she had begun euphemistically calling Alex's seizure, Loriah and Clint had raced their son to the nearest hospital. Alex had been unconscious the entire time, reviving only after twelve hours in the hospital's ICU. A barrage of doctors, residents, and various nurses and assistants had smothered, covered, and stuffed him with medications, IVs, tubes, and needles.

When Alex opened his eyes yesterday morning, they were peach-colored and filmy.

Test after test after test failed to pinpoint the cause of Alex's sudden illness. One doctor had been especially enthusiastic about the idea of organic phosphate poisoning, while another had been confident that it was as-yet undiagnosed epilepsy. Yet another offered a zebra of a diagnosis: hereditary hemorrhagic telangiectasia, a bleeding disorder that can appear at any age.

They were all wrong, but Loriah wasn't as scared as she'd been yesterday. Alex was awake, he was eating, and he seemed normal.

"Mom, what's wrong?" The sound of her son's voice, still raspy from the tube the doctors had shoved down his throat while he was unconscious, jolted Loriah out of her reverie.

"What do you mean, honey?"

"You just had this weird look on your face."

"Oh." Loriah couldn't think of anything else to say.

Alex smiled. "I'm going to be okay, Mom. Really. I feel fine now."

Loriah let out a shaky breath. "I know, honey." But she didn't, not really—Alex's eyes still looked like sharp little kumquats and she hoped against hope that the slight redness she noticed around his neck wasn't the start of some sort of rash.

"Do you think I can go home today?" Alex spooned more gleaming potato salad into his mouth.

"I'm not sure, sweetie—we'll have to ask Dr. Briggs when she comes back."

Alex shrugged. "Eh, no worries. It's not too bad here. Especially since they have my favorite food." Alex grinned and gestured toward Loriah with a potato salad-filled spoon. "I still can't believe MY mom made this and now everybody's eating it!"

Loriah waved a hand in a show of humility. "Oh, honey—it wasn't just me. I have a really good team at Natural Light."

Alex beamed. He really was a very good boy. "Well, I'm really proud of you, Mom."

She glanced down to hide her tear-filled eyes from her son. "Thank you, honey. Your father and I love you very much."

She glanced back up.

That was definitely a rash on Alex's neck.

And his lips were turning blue.

And he was gasping for air.

Loriah screamed.

* * *

Another twelve hours had passed since Alex's second 'episode.' Hearing her scream, doctors and nurses had flooded into the room, initiating lifesaving protocols, clearing his airway again, and rushing him away for more tests as soon as they felt he was stable.

Loriah waited like a sentinel in Alex's room, staring at his empty bed. She called Clint at work, told him what had happened. He offered to meet her at the hospital and relieve her for a while so she could get some sleep, but she refused. She wouldn't leave Alex for a single minute.

But, she was going to go insane if she had to keep staring at those stale, rumpled bed sheets—wondering if, sometime soon, all the rooms of her heart would contain permanently empty beds, the Alex-shaped dent fading more each day. So, she distracted herself with work.

She pulled up her work email on her phone and started sorting: quick deletions for spam and unnecessary forwards or chain emails, flags for things she would look at later, and quick responses to simple questions. She almost started humming as she worked, nearly forgetting where she was. Until she came to an email from her colleague Steve marked *Urgent*. The subject line: READ THIS NOW.

Her fingers shook slightly as she opened Steve's email. The body of the message read:

Dr. Harp,

I'm contacting you immediately regarding troubling results with the lab mice. As we discussed, I've been following an acetylsterolstearate murine feeding protocol to study the effects of different doses of the chemical.

The experimental groups receiving the three highest dosage levels of acetylsterolstearate have started exhibiting symptoms consistent with allergy or poisoning. So far, I've cataloged bleeding from facial orifices, weight loss, mild hair loss, and mild difficulty breathing. One mouse in the highest dosage group has died. In contrast, all of the control group mice are healthy and exhibit normal functioning.

I'm especially troubled because, as we calculated, the three highest dosage levels are well within range of what we estimated the average American is consuming now.

Please call me as soon as you receive this.

Steve

Now Loriah was the one with difficulty breathing. The murine symptoms sounded sickeningly similar to her son's...and if ASS was causing this, and one mouse had even died already...combined with the fact that Alex had been drowning all his food in Natural Light Mayo for the past six months...

Loriah turned her head and promptly vomited into a pink plastic trashcan.

How could she save him? Was there even a way? And if she did succeed, how could she warn the others? The millions of Americans shoveling down Natural Light every day...

* * *

Jeff Richardson, Natural Light Foods' CEO, laughed. Directly in Loriah's face.

"Dr. Harp. Please. Speak reasonably, now."

"Jeff—"

"No, no. There's no way we're pulling our number one seller, which, might I remind you, has made the company and YOU PERSONALLY millions of dollars, from the shelves just because one sick mouse died and a few others have a little rash. Are you crazy?"

Steve piped up from his seat next to Loriah. "Mr.

Richardson, it's true that only one mouse died, but the others don't have just a little rash. They're all bleeding from the nose, eyes, mouth, anus—"

Jeff waved a hand dismissively. "So, we got a bad batch of mice."

Steve's face darkened. "The experimental mice were from the same breeder as the control mice, and that group is entirely healthy."

"So? Even if that's true, and I'm not saying it is, then that doesn't mean humans will be affected just because mice are. As you both well know, humans and mice are very different."

Loriah cringed at Jeff's patronizing tone. "Jeff. It isn't just the mice. You know very well that my son has been hospitalized for over a week now with the same symptoms as the mice."

Jeff's face softened—but only slightly. His tone was gentler as he said, "Loriah. You know I'm very sorry about your son. But the boy may just have an allergy! Who knows what we put into our bodies these days?"

Loriah exploded. "WE do. WE are the ones who know what we put into our bodies! WE fucking make the shit! My son, just like so many other people, has been eating Natural Light Mayo like it's water and he's dying of thirst. *That's not a fucking coincidence.*"

"Loriah," Jeff growled, all gentleness evaporated. "Watch your language. There is nothing wrong with our mayonnaise."

"Mr. Richardson, have you not searched the web recently?" Steve asked. "There are more and more chat forums and articles talking about the 'mysterious allergy' popping up all over the country. People are starting to make the connection. They're starting to ask questions."

"I don't fucking care!" Jeff roared. "Maybe they should think about making better choices and losing weight if they really care about their health!"

"Jeff. You have kids. Think about the parents feeding this to their families!" Loriah said.

Jeff laughed again, the sound fierce like a gunshot. "Are you serious, Loriah? I would never eat this myself, much less feed this shit to my kids."

"JEFF. I feed this to MY family. How can you sell a product you won't eat yourself?"

"I can do it because it makes a shit ton of money! Wake up, Loriah! This is the real fucking world. Let's look at the facts. We're not getting any shit from the FDA. There aren't any *Wall Street Journal* or *New York Fucking Times* articles calling us out. No inspectors or reporters or even Susie fucking Homemakers are sniffing around, so who cares if a few internet trolls are whining from their moms' basements? All of this means: we're A-OKAY."

"But this poison mayo could be *killing children*." Loriah's voice sliced through the air.

Jeff leaned forward, stood up, and placed both greasy hands on the smooth glass of the conference table. His dark eyes smoldered. "Dr. Harp. Dr. Billings. Let me make this very clear. There is nothing wrong with our product. And unless somebody spontaneously combusts after eating our mayo, I'm. Not. Pulling it."

Jeff raked a hand through his slicked-back hair and marched from the room.

* * *

"Mom?"

Loriah awoke with a start, her eyes fuzzy with dream afterimages of Alex's corpse, laid out in a coffin. A tear spilled down her cheek, mixing with the nightmare sweat trickling from her brow. "Alex?"

"Mom, I'm thirsty," Alex croaked.

Loriah handed him a large pink plastic thermos of water with a hospital-issue bendy straw. He slurped weakly, his eyes wandering to look out the window. A light rain had begun to fall.

After he'd had his second episode, the doctors ran every reasonable test; they even ran a few of them twice. When those all came back negative or otherwise inconclusive, they started running the unreasonable tests. They were still awaiting results from the latest round of tests, and for the past week, Alex had hovered in a semi-conscious state. Loriah had barely left his bedside, and Clint joined her in the evenings when he finished work.

"How are you feeling today, honey?"

Alex slurped some more, coughed. "I'm okay. Not great, but not terrible, either."

"Is there anything I can get for you? Games? Food? One of your books from home?" Loriah's eyes were desperate; she felt so helpless in the presence of her son's illness. In the dark center of her heart, that helplessness mingled with guilt; she was now sure that her mayonnaise was doing this to her only child. And she had even smiled as she squirted it onto his plate.

But she wasn't blind anymore. No mayonnaise had touched Alex's lips since she had opened that email about the mouse results from Steve.

"Nah, it's okay, Mom. The only thing I would really want is some more mayo. They stopped putting it on my tray."

Loriah's lips trembled. "I'm sorry honey, but I don't think that's a good idea right now."

Alex looked up, his brow furrowed in confusion. "Why not?"

"You know, with your condition and all...we need you to heal."

"But I thought the mayo was healthy?"

Loriah paused. "Um—"

"You wouldn't let me eat something that wasn't good for me, right, Mom?" Alex's tone conveyed a youthful hopefulness and the confidence of somebody asking a question they already knew the answer to.

A flicker of anguish twisted across Loriah's pale face. Quietly, she said: "Not if I knew it."

* * *

A blank legal pad stared up at Loriah, its yellowness mirroring the sallow shade her skin had developed after a week at her son's bedside. Alex was having more tests done, and the nurses had urged Loriah to go home, take a shower, and get some sleep.

She'd done two of those things. She was home, at her desk, and her hair was clean for the first time in a week. But sleep eluded her, and a swirl of angry, terrified thoughts corkscrewed like a tornado in her mind.

Jeff would never voluntarily pull the mayo. And if she pushed him any harder, she'd only succeed in getting herself fired and losing any power she might have to keep people safe from the demon she'd midwifed onto their dinner plates.

She needed to brainstorm ideas—thus, the mocking legal pad. She sighed, and her fingers gripped tight on the pen, as though trying to squeeze ideas out of it through brute force. Exhaustion pounded in her eyeballs, but she knew she wouldn't be able to rest.

Pen in hand, she began by numbering a list down the page. The pad looked a little friendlier now, and Loriah's shoulders relaxed a fraction of an inch. She wrote:

1. Ignore everything going on with the mayo and just never feed it to my family again.
2. Somehow pretend to be Jeff and give the recall order myself.
3. Tip off the FDA.
4. 'Borrow' the mouse lab results—and give them to the press.

Number one was never really an option—after the agony she endured while Alex was sick, she couldn't imagine leaving other parents to that fate. Number two would have serious, possibly criminal, consequences. Plus, she wasn't sure how she could actually impersonate Jeff. Number three was not a horrible option, but Loriah knew from experience that the FDA was slow moving and didn't have very sharp teeth.

That left...number four. Jeff himself had said that no major news outlets were calling them out, which meant everything was fine. If Loriah were to change that...Jeff wouldn't have much of a choice. Pro: poison mayo would be removed from the shelves, potentially saving countless lives. Con: Loriah would definitely be fired.

She set down the pen and legal pad and dressed smartly, as if she were headed to the office. This might be the last time she'd be allowed there, so why not leave a good impression?

After all, she'd rather be fired a hundred times over than have another child's blood on her hands.

* * *

This wasn't a movie, so there were no close calls or avoidable mishaps. No nosy coworkers or overzealous security guards. She simply walked into the office, accessed the mouse lab results on her work computer, copied them to a flash drive, and put the flash drive in her purse. Then she walked out, waving to Steve as she went.

* * *

With the flash drive in her purse, Loriah drove back to the hospital. The nurse had called—apparently Alex's new tests found something more conclusive.

She really didn't want to blow up her career so spectacularly. She didn't want to be a sneaky whistleblower—but what else was left when she eliminated the impossible options? Everything narrowed down to a single question: would she let people die, or not?

And when it all came down to that, it wasn't much of a choice at all.

Alex's final lab tests gave her more surety than anything else could.

"We've found something," the pleasant, plump nurse in pink scrubs said. Her ID badge read 'Elena.'

Loriah crossed her legs in her chair, looked at her son lying placidly in the bed. "Alright," she said, trying to still the shake in her voice. "What is it?"

"Our last round of tests with Alex were a specific subset of allergy tests. We had him write down all of the foods he eats on a regular basis, and we based the testing agents off of that list." Elena paused.

"Okay," Loriah said. She could sense that the nurse was dreading this conversation. "Then what happened?"

The pink scrubs rumpled on the hunched shoulders of their nervous owner. "The only food agent that provoked a reaction—and this was a very strong reaction—was—" Elena paused again, her eyes terrified.

Loriah grew impatient. "Well, for God's sake, what is making my son so sick?"

The nurse took a deep breath, her face resigned. With a shrug, she said, "Mayonnaise."

* * *

There was no point in trying to be covert about it—Jeff would find her out in zero seconds flat. Then he would sue the shit out of her for violating her NDA. But, with the money all that mayo made her, she could afford a good lawyer. That seemed fitting, somehow.

Because she was reasonably attractive and was comfortable speaking to other humans instead of just lab equipment, Loriah had been consulted throughout the years by various media outlets to comment on food-related policies and procedures. She hadn't done much of that in a couple of years, but she knew for a fact that one of her old contacts, a reporter for the *New York Times* named Fiona White, was still around. She'd read Fiona's recent articles on the *E. coli* outbreak in romaine and had been enchanted by the woman's ability to make something unsettling but drily scientific sound so compelling. Fiona was the right choice for this story.

Fiona's office number was still in Loriah's phone, and she

called it immediately after excusing herself from the room still holding Elena and her son. In the hospital hallway, she made the most self-destructive but necessary call of her life.

Fiona answered after the first ring. "Dr. Harp! Is that you?"

Loriah's voice trembled. "Hi, Fiona! Yes, it's me."

"Wow, it's been a while, huh?" Fiona's voice was congenial.

"It has, it has." Loriah paused to collect herself—tears scratched at the back of her eyeballs.

When she didn't go on, Fiona prodded, "So, what do you have for me, Dr. Harp?"

"Please, Fiona—call me Loriah."

"Alright, what have you got for me, Loriah?"

Loriah swallowed past a large, persistent lump in her throat. No point beating around the bush now. "Our mayonnaise is poison," she said flatly.

There was silence on the end of the line.

"Fiona? Hello?"

Loriah heard a cough. Then, Fiona's startled voice: "What?"

"You know, Natural Light Foods mayonnaise? Well, there's a food additive in it—we've been marketing it pretty heavily. It's called acetylsterolstearate...You probably know it as ASS."

"Right, right," Fiona whispered.

"Well. A recent batch of mouse experiments have shown that high levels of ASS consumption can be poisonous. Even fatal."

Fiona gasped so forcefully that Loriah was sure she'd punctured a lung.

"And there's more," Loriah said.

"Oh dear God."

"My son. He's been in the hospital for over a week now, after he had a seizure and collapsed on our dining table. Then he started bleeding and having trouble breathing."

"Oh my God, Loriah—I'm so sorry."

"It's okay now. The doctors ran a last batch of tests. Allergy tests. Want to guess what he's reacting so violently to?" The sarcasm in Loriah's voice was tinged with an iron-bitter anger.

"Mayonnaise," Fiona breathed.

"Bingo."

There was a brief silence on the line. Loriah could hear the wheels in Fiona's brain turning, ramping up for what could be the story of her career.

How ironic, Loriah thought. *What makes her career will end mine.*

"How much information can you give me?" Fiona asked.

"I have the mouse lab results on a flash drive and I'll disclose my son's allergy test results as long as you leave his name, and mine, completely out of this."

"Done and done. Can you overnight the flash drive?"

"I'm on my way to FedEx right now."

"That's perfect. Thank you, Loriah. I'm sure this was a difficult decision."

Loriah sighed, overcome with weariness now that her role in this clusterfuck was nearing its end. "It wasn't, though. When I saw my son lying in that bed, threaded through with tubes, I knew I couldn't do that to another person's child." Loriah sighed again. "Oh, and Fiona?"

"Yes?"

"Throw out all your mayo."

"Dumping it into the trash as we speak."

* * *

Alex got better. Now that they knew what they were dealing with, the doctors gave him a new type of antihistamine that calmed his violent allergy symptoms. And, of course—they cut all mayo from his diet. They hadn't cut it from all hospital dining options—but Loriah knew that they would, as soon as Fiona's article was published.

And when that article did come out, three days later (wow, Fiona sure put the rush on that one, God bless her), it might as well have been a harbinger of the apocalypse given the public outcry.

As you can imagine, Loriah was fired. Jeff had a security guard present during that meeting, not so much for legal reasons as for the simple fact that Jeff knew that being in a room alone with her was dangerous—his hands were making involuntarily gripping gestures that would fit nicely around Loriah's whistleblowing throat.

And then there was the flurry of lawsuits. Jeff/Natural Light Foods sued Loriah, Steve sued Jeff, and millions of consumers—every John, Jane, and Joe who had been feeling a bit under the weather lately—sued Natural Light. The FDA came down hard on the company, and the board fired Jeff.

And then the board had to basically go fuck off because between the lawsuits, the settlements, the public relations nightmare, the FDA investigation, and the loss of billions of dollars' worth of product, Natural Light had to declare bankruptcy.

ASS mayonnaise didn't get to poison anybody else.

* * *

You're probably thinking: but what happened next? Did Loriah get out of Jeff's lawsuit unscathed? Did Alex really stay better? What about Fiona, or Steve?

Well, I can't answer all of your questions, but I'll try. Loriah did indeed hire a damn good lawyer, who argued that Loriah had been acting in favor of the public good when she gave the mouse results to a reporter. Luckily for Loriah (and for Steve's pending lawsuit against Jeff), Steve had recorded their earlier meeting with the prickly CEO. They had proof that Jeff knew ASS was bad but shoved it into consumers' mouths anyway.

But, of course, Loriah did steal company property and publish it. She did violate her NDA. But the judge was sympathetic—her own daughter had developed a rash after eating two helpings of creamy potato salad. In the end, Loriah had to pay a small pittance to Jeff and to (the nearly extinct) Natural Light Foods. With the rest of her mayo money she paid her lawyer and then set up a nonprofit public interest group with the express purpose of monitoring and publicizing, when necessary, the dangers of food additives.

Steve won his lawsuit, and was awarded $5 million. He contributed half to Loriah's nonprofit.

Alex really did stay better. He never touched mayo again, even regular, non-Natural Light mayo. The bleeding stopped, his breathing returned to normal, and he didn't have another seizure. He played soccer in the fall and broke all sorts of school records.

Fiona parlayed her blockbuster article into a book deal.

Her book, *Mayonnaise*, won a Pulitzer and topped the *New York Times* Bestseller list for twenty-two weeks in a row. She donated a large portion of her profits to Loriah's organization.

Mayonnaise is now being made into a movie, which is probably why you were curious about how this all happened in real life. I should let you know that some of the actors aren't actors at all—Loriah is playing herself, as are Steve and Fiona. Alex has gotten older, and can't really pass for a kid anymore, but he's on set every day during his summer break from college to support his mom.

Oh, and the craft table doesn't have a single drop of mayonnaise.

* * *

This story first appeared in the After Dinner Conversation—June 2020 issue.

Discussion Questions

1. Why do people buy "light" or "zero calorie" food and drinks? Is it really as simple as "they want more, but don't want to be overweight," or is there something else individually, or culturally, going on?
2. Before being released to the public, should a new product (*food additive, car, soft drink, cell phone, etc.*) have to prove that it is safe, or should it be on the market until it is proven dangerous? What is our current system?
3. What do you think Loriah's response to the email would have been if she had read it, but no one she knew had personally gotten sick? Is Loriah a "good person" or just a person with a personal story?
4. Given that companies (*as an entity*) can never have a "personal story" with a product the way Loriah did, can a company ever be expected to respond the way Loriah did?
5. Does the fact that the company lost billions of dollars, declared bankruptcy, and likely had to lay off thousands of employees matter at all in determining the best course? Does it matter that many naturally occurring foods you can buy in the store, when eaten in sufficient amounts (*or in certain ways*), can also kill you?

* * *

Bugs In the Valley

Saba Waheed

* * *

"So, did you fix nature?" I leaned over the stool at the bar.
"Excuse me?"

"Ethics class," I said. Amaya stared at me blankly.
"Stanford," I continued, "you argued science for the greater
good means editing genes to improve humanity, population
control to preserve resources. Nature botched the job…"

"And we should fix it," Amaya said, her expression still
stoic. "Right, you called me a eugenicist."

I smiled but she merely turned back to her drink. She had
the same loner energy I remembered from college. I never saw
her at parties, or academic clubs, never saw her date anyone. I'd
see her walking alone, her head leaning slightly forward as if her
mind was already at the destination. Amaya was the kind of
beautiful that didn't know she was, or didn't care.

"You were right." I motioned to the bartender for another
drink. "If we have the resources to design a better world, then
we should do it."

"I'm always right," she said without turning to me. I took my drink and went back to the table with my work team. I watched as Amaya remained at the bar alone the rest of the night. She didn't use her phone, she didn't read anything, she never even glanced back to see who else was in the bar. She just looked forward, finishing one drink after another.

When I said goodbye to the last of my friends, I went back to the bar.

"You work in the Valley?"

"Yes."

"Yeah, me too." I waited for her to say more, but nothing. "Tech? Business?"

"Medical."

"What company?"

"Can't say."

"I work in tech. Not R&D, but the business side. My team and I were celebrating tonight. We got driverless cars approved statewide."

For the first time, she turned and looked at me. "I thought that program was dead."

"It was." I sat down on the stool and told her my strategies—reshape the conversation, get buy-in from politicians, override regulation, create some new laws, repeat.

"One day my work will be ready for the world," she said. When she looked at me, it felt like she was taking all of me with her. Then she turned away and the feeling was gone. She signaled to the bartender and asked for her check. It was abrupt. "Good chatting." She put down the cash and walked away.

Later that week I used my connections to figure out where she worked. When I discovered it was Gamelin, one of the most heavily invested medical labs in the Valley, I knew she was working on something big. A few weeks later, Amaya reached out to me.

I arrived at a local cafe and found her already seated. "I hear you're the best and can get anything to the market." I was pleased my reputation had caught her attention. "Join my team."

"You haven't told me what you do."

"You have to say yes first."

My success in the Valley was knowing when to jump.

I went through a series of background checks, non-disclosure agreements, and interviews. Once approved, Amaya asked me to attend a briefing for the company's board and top investors. Her assistant loaded up the presentation and Amaya steadily went through their work. They built medical nanotech, an application she referred to simply as 'the bugs', that could safely enter the body.

"Have you ever seen those tanks with fish that eat away the dead skin on your feet?" Her gaze landed on me and I smiled. "They have the ability to go after dead cells while leaving the healthy ones behind. Our bugs do the same. They roam through the body until they find a malignant tumor and then eat away at it until it's gone."

When the presentation was over, the room lit up. "We cured cancer! We did it."

"Wait, wait, there's one more thing." The board quieted and turned back to Amaya. "The bugs cannot be permitted to stay in the body. They themselves continue to replicate to a point where they can take over and become a sort of plague. So, we program them to die after a few replications and the body disposes of them. In all of our cases to date, the cancer returns."

"It's temporary?" asked one of the board members.

"Yes, but it works for years, anywhere from five to ten years. That's a lot of time with family, and far better quality of life, not stuck in chemo or radiation."

"Why not inject them again?" asked another board member.

"There's a limited supply and until we can figure that part out, our strategy is to spread it out, broaden the benefits." This is when she looked right at me. "Let's give more people a few more good years, rather than give only a few people many more years."

I met Amaya later to develop the plan. She told me how she'd started to build the technology when she was in graduate school. It had worked in animals and that success got her a position and a ridiculous amount of money and resources at the Gamelin Lab. But, for years, no matter what she did, the human body rejected the bugs.

"The technology alone wasn't enough, so I started doing all kinds of animal and plant experiments." She'd brought in geologists, environmentalists, herbalists, zoologists, and botanists and told them to bring in anything that could mimic cells.

"Nature."

"Yes," she smiled. "We needed nature. I met a plant specialist who brought me rare plants from around the world. One plant, ironically called the 'corpse flower,' worked. It gave the bugs an organic cover and the human body didn't see them as invaders. But the plant only exists in one part of the world, and we haven't figured out how to grow it here in the lab. But we will."

Amaya's project gave me new focus. My team created the distribution strategy. A project like this would take years to reach the public but I leveraged every single one of my contacts to fast track the process. Amaya would meet with me regularly to discuss the approach. She wanted it to reach patients with the least access to treatment. It was during one of these meetings that she told me how both her parents died.

"Freshman year of college. Cancer. One right after the other." She was sitting in an office chair across from me. It was a moment of vulnerability I hadn't seen in her. "Thanks, nature."

"That's why you were so..."

"I was so what?" She looked up, a wall back up.

"Nothing."

I shocked the entire Valley when I lined up all the necessary approvals in three months. We held a press conference and had media from every part of the country, every part of the world. None of my tech projects had received this kind of exposure. Amaya and I celebrated over drinks that night. She was glowing. She looked at me with such fullness and light. "You did it," she said.

"We did it," I replied. We were at a bar, sitting on stools side by side. "Our world is better off with all the new technologies. Streets are safer, we have more access to food, and now this—bugs that can fight nature's greatest threat to our bodies."

"I just need to make it bigger. I'm close. I can feel it." Then she turned to me and said abruptly. "Come home with me."

And I did.

A few weeks later we found out she was pregnant. I thought back to that night and the details were fuzzy. Were we careful, was I too drunk to care, had she encouraged me to go forward anyway? "I want to do this," she said, when we met to discuss what to do. "I won't make the time otherwise. I have no expectations of you. We can make it contractual, so you're in the clear."

"I want to do it." I said it before I had fully processed what that meant.

I was in the hospital room when Jayde was born. I laid her on my chest and I couldn't feel the difference in our bodies. I looked at this little being that was part me and part Amaya and the world felt whole. Amaya took time off from work and it was probably the only extended period she had ever spent away from her project. I would come over in the evenings, relieving her so she could rest. By the time Jayde was five, I had moved in and we were functioning as a family.

As Jayde grew, so did her curiosity. One day we were out sitting in a neighborhood park. It was a warm Saturday afternoon. Amaya was in the lab and I had taken the day off. "What does Mama do?"

"Your mama, she's the brains behind the bugs."

"Ew." Jayde scowled.

"No, these are super bugs that kill the bad guy cells."

"And what do you do?"

"I create the path for the bugs to go from the lab into our bodies." Jayde looked at me questioningly. "You see that coffeebot that knew exactly what I wanted to drink before I even walked up? People were afraid of robots and didn't want them making our drinks or cleaning our homes. I changed that, changed the way people think about machines and what they are willing to accept. Now, look, they are everywhere."

As the years passed, our inboxes were filled with messages from individuals and family members. Amaya would bring a few home and we would sit down with Jayde in the evenings and read them together. But I could feel Amaya's frustration in not being able to get those families more time, and not being able to get the bugs to more families.

She wasn't the only one feeling impatient.

In the tenth year of the program, one of the project investors came to my office. "The whole thing is a money pit." I knew this already. The hospital program didn't generate revenue and the production and research was costly. "We can give it a year, after that, the research ends, and we put the bugs on the market."

I told Amaya about the meeting. "If it goes on the market, only some people will have access to it—people like my parents would be left out." There was desperation in her voice. "I can't make the science go any faster."

I couldn't handle seeing Amaya so upset. I reached out to the investor to negotiate more time. When I got to his office, he was sitting with another man wearing a lab coat—Amaya's number two.

"We will fund the project if you change the business plan." He pushed forward a new non-disclosure agreement. If I shared anything about our deal, the entire project would be defunded— the research, the production, the patients. If I didn't sign it, the entire project would be defunded in a year anyway. "You can't tell Amaya," he repeated as I signed.

He directed me to the lab. A technician took me into a plain room with a table and two chairs. She pulled up my sleeve, swabbed it with alcohol and, with an unusually large syringe, injected me. "That's it?" I asked. It was less than a prick. Over the next few weeks, I started to feel slight changes. I could run a little faster, my mind felt clearer, and I could feel a whirlpool of energy throughout my body.

I went back to the investor's office.

"You get it now, right?"

"I get that something is happening."

Amaya's number two explained it. "A few years into the project, we noticed that people who had the bug, it wasn't just that the cancer was gone, they were getting healthier than they were before. There was a youthfulness that came back, and parts of the body that had been aging, reversed. It turns out, the bugs weren't stopping at the cancer, they were zipping through the system repairing everything—from organs to decomposing cells."

"Meaning?"

"There's never a moment of cellular senescence. The bugs keep you healthy and they keep you young."

"Amaya's known for some years about this 'side effect'," the investor said.

"Why are you telling me this?"

"You're the best strategist we have," he said, leaning back in his chair. "And, you'll do anything to make sure the project survives."

He was right. I rounded up a dozen billionaires from the Valley and beyond. When they heard what the bug could do, one of them turned to the Gamelin Lab investor and asked, "You built an anti-aging bug?" The investor nodded, a huge grin on his face.

He stood up, as if giving a toast. "Friends, here we are, on the cusp of change. To everlasting life!" The room crowed in delight.

I was miserable holding this back from Amaya but a few days later, she came home and told me that her budget had increased. "Whatever you did, thank you," she said.

As the months turned into a year and a year into many, my body had changed, or rather, it stopped changing. Don't get me wrong, a bus could still run me over, and the bugs would do nothing for that. But my body was healthy and without the specter of aging and disease, I felt bigger, stronger, and became less risk-averse. With a few more billionaires, I garnered even more resources. I eyed other companies, finding the top developers and scientists at the forefront of new ideas and technology, and bought them.

Amaya and I became distant. She went into a dark hole every time she failed to replicate the corpse flower. Meanwhile, I was on the rise, and was bringing more and more technologies into the public. I was the most sought-after person in the Valley.

When Jayde was ready for college, she chose an art school in New York. I was disappointed. I thought she would follow one of our careers. Amaya and I took a few days off to settle her into her dorm. We explored the city and ate meals at different restaurants. It should have been a joyful family trip, but Amaya snapped at me and grew more irritable as the weekend went by.

She was quiet on the way back, staring out the plane window even though it was dark. When we got home, I made myself a drink. Amaya watched me from the kitchen counter. The silence between us was enormous.

She finally spoke. "Who told you?"

"Told me what?" I said as I took a full swig of the whiskey, clearing half the glass. "Why didn't you tell me?"

"I didn't tell anyone."

"I am not anyone. You should've trusted me."

"I was right not to."

"You weren't complaining when your budget increased." I looked at her sideways and I could tell she was brimming with anger.

"And what was the purpose of you taking it?"

I was surprised that she knew. "I needed to understand how it worked," I mumbled.

She went into her bag and pulled out a reader. She pushed aside my drink and placed it in front of me. It was a message from a mother whose daughter Nori was diagnosed with stage four brain cancer. Even with all the science today, she had only weeks. "That dose in you could've given that mother another decade with her daughter."

I scrolled down and noticed her place on the waitlist. "She's next in line for the bugs."

"She's dead." Amaya stepped back. "No more doses for you or the others."

"Then your project is dead," I said. Her face contorted and I saw that she knew I was right. She walked out of the kitchen and I heard the bedroom door slam.

I slept in the guest bedroom. I believed once we got some rest, we could talk about it again. When I woke up and walked into the kitchen, she was already drinking coffee. "I want you to move out."

"Look, I know I shouldn't have taken it."

"Out," she said without any emotions.

"It was only once."

Amaya didn't respond. She got up, grabbed her bag and left for work. I went to a hotel and figured we'd talk about it after a few days. But she refused to return my messages and they wouldn't let me into the lab to see her.

The doses the investors received were ending. I could feel the bugs leaving my system. My body felt heavy, weighed down by gravity. I felt lethargic and my mind was cluttering up. Worst of all, my emotions were palpable. I needed to talk to Amaya and we had to figure this out. If we didn't renew the doses, I didn't see how we could continue the project. Now that she knew, I wanted to work together with her to find a solution. I waited outside of our house. When she saw me, her face glowed with anger.

"We have to talk," I said.

"People died because of you."

"And many more are going to live because of me."

"You have an overblown understanding of your importance."

"Look, just listen to me, we have to figure out what to do next."

"There is no 'we' in this project. The bugs are mine."

"They aren't yours."

"You. You are...just some middle man."

Now I was angry. "What did you see in me anyway?"

"You...you just happened." She pushed past me and went into the unit. I hated her at that moment. Something was finally stripped away and I was seeing Amaya for who she was—she didn't care for anything but the bugs.

The next day, I went back to the lab and got a new dose. As soon as they pushed the syringe, I felt big again. I knew it wasn't possible, the bugs didn't move that fast, but even the idea that they were there, fortifying my body, gave me strength.

And with the bugs inside of me, Amaya mattered less.

I renewed another round of the bugs to the billionaires to keep Amaya's project funded. I still believed in its mission even if she didn't believe in me. But I brought in additional donors to support my expansion into other sectors. I was taking over more companies, buying up all the patents so that all new tech had to go through me. I placed some friendly faces in city councils, state and federal governments. The tech world was thriving and I was leading the charge.

I shouldn't have been surprised when the media leak happened. I suspected Amaya. Journalists reported that the bug program had shifted from hospitals to wealthy clients. Protesters staged demonstrations outside of our offices and labs, demanding justice. "Bugs for the sick, not for the rich." I worked with our security to take care of it. We could access their plans through any one of their home or handheld devices and countered or preempted their actions. When a few of the protest leaders received a dose of bugs, they quickly backed off. We initiated a public lottery program—to bring in a few non-elites. You didn't have to have cancer, or be rich, to get the bugs.

I could imagine Amaya's rage, but I wasn't around to witness it.

The next time I saw her was in the boardroom. She had sprinkles of white hair that shined under the light. A part of me hoped she'd take the bugs, even if just to fight me for a few more years. When it was time to present her findings to the board, she stood at the edge of the conference table, looked around the room and then said that there were no new updates. They had failed again to replicate the corpse flower.

Amaya kept her eyes moving, scanning each of the faces. When she got to mine, she stopped. She stared at me, and I saw recognition in her eyes. She knew that I knew that she was lying. She dared me to say something. I dropped my gaze and she moved on.

Afterwards, I saw her in the hallway. "Why didn't you tell them about the breakthrough?"

"They don't deserve the bugs."

As she turned to walk away, I grabbed her arm. "You will lose this project if you don't tell them."

"I will lose this project if I tell them."

A few weeks later, I was walking by the bar, the one where we first ran into each other decades ago now. Amaya was sitting alone, her drink mostly full. Maybe she felt me because she turned around and our eyes met. I saw something in her face, something familiar. Buried under all that rage, what we had, it was there. It was still there. I moved to open the door but she turned away, back to her drink.

I came home to my empty unit. There were women I could call but I didn't feel like it. I put my bag and jacket down and powered down all the bots and gadgets. The wind was pounding against the windows, the night rageful. I grabbed a beer and some cheese out of the fridge, and pulled out a box of crackers. At the kitchen counter, I ate quietly. Maybe I was nearing the end of a dose. Maybe a disease had found its way into my body and the bugs were working harder. Or maybe, it was seeing Amaya.

I was the most powerful man in the Valley, but I felt like I had just landed at the bottom of a pit. I got into bed and couldn't sleep. My mind was racing, searching for a way to turn this around. With sufficient supply, we wouldn't have to choose anymore. I needed Amaya to listen to me. I felt my eyes grow heavy just as the sun was coming up. As I was about to finally fall asleep, I was bombarded by a series of alerts in my ear implant.

Amaya had died in a lab explosion.

The FBI was at the site by the time I arrived. They told me that Amaya and a lab technician were working early that morning. There was some kind of accident and both of them died. Only part of the lab was harmed but it was the side that held the components needed to replicate the flower. Amaya had cordoned off staff access to the research long ago so that no one knew the whole process. They would have to start over.

The next day, an FBI agent was sitting at my desk flipping through a series of photos, messages and documents. The agent said that they had evidence that Amaya was planning to blow up the lab but the technician caught her. He was able to subvert the operation. He sacrificed his life to save the lab. She was attempting to destroy the research and entire production infrastructure for the bugs.

"That's not possible, she lived for the program," I said.

"Our understanding, sir, is that the company was going to take the program away from her after she replicated the flower. They had already alerted us to the possibility of her doing something like this."

It was no accident.

Amaya's name was now associated with terrorists.

Not the founder of the bugs.

I went to visit Jayde. She didn't believe any of the news reports, and I didn't have the heart to tell her about the evidence.

We held a private memorial and spent a few mournful days together. I took the cross-country bullet train home. I sat in the cocktail lounge. It was set up retro style with ornate sofas and tables. Classical music played softly in the background. I found a seat in a booth by a window. The BarBot came by and I ordered a whiskey on the rocks. I took a sip and turned my head to the side to look outside. We were going so fast that the landscape was a blur and yet the ride was smooth. The bullet train was one of my company's initiatives. I had moved so many stalled projects, brought technology to a new apex. The bugs made it possible. I made it happen. Here I was running circles around Amaya's righteousness but she never saw what I was doing. I looked around the cabin. No one was complaining.

I went back for a new dose of the bug. We revised our distribution system. There were tiers, 1-dose, 3-doses, 5-doses and so on which we would use strategically. We distributed to businessmen, to heads of states—I believed it brought peace and kept commerce strong. Nothing stopped war like bugs.

Jayde and I became closer after Amaya's death. We met regularly and it was during one of her art exhibits that I realized that she was becoming older than me. I offered her the bugs.

"I don't know. Do I want to extend my life?"

"It's not about living longer, it's the clarity and succinctness of that living. You won't be muddled by fear. You will stay you, but a more effective you."

Jayde gave me a considering look. "But mom never took it."

"It was a different time then."

"How many artists have it?"

"You'd be the first."

The next wave of public backlash was bigger. People complained that we were using the bugs to manipulate politics, fast track our own projects, and distribute resources unevenly, leaving people at the bottom suffering. The newest round of resistance was harder to quell. They were leaderless and we couldn't quite figure out who to detain or retain with bugs. Instead, we did a broad scramble of public communications and built a counter media campaign—the public understood that centralizing the bugs is what brought them the conveniences and technological advances.

What I didn't expect was Jayde's sympathy for them. She visited me via hologram at my office one afternoon. "You're misusing the bugs." She stood there like Amaya's ghost.

"Jayde, don't make accusations," I said dismissively.

"You called the military on protesters."

"What, who told you that?" We'd had a hard media blackout on that approach.

"Is it true?" When I didn't respond, she phased out.

Jayde continued to fight with me and started to cancel on our monthly dinners. When we would meet, she'd insist that the bug program was corrupt.

"You're being manipulated," I told her.

"I have the mental clarity that came with the bugs," she retorted. It was true and that is what surprised me. With the bugs, I thought she would understand them and their power. Instead, she was becoming the spokesperson for their end.

She joined Back to the Basics, a radical group of luddites that wanted to slow down tech and science and end the bugs program. She removed all tech gadgets from her life making it impossible for me to track her. I thought she would come back when she needed a new dose, and that by then the rebelliousness would end.

The years moved slower after Jayde cut off communication with me. Even with the bugs, I felt a kind of heaviness. I thought of having another child, and had been in relationships where that was possible, but it was never about kids, it was about Jayde. It was harder to stay engaged. The world consisted of just a few companies that were being run by those of us on the bugs.

I felt my first bit of joy in a decade when Jayde reached out. I met her on a farm plot in the South. She laid in a bare and simple room. Each strand of white hair, each wrinkle signaled her departure. I begged her to take the bugs, "We can have a few more years together."

"No," she said simply. "You get off them."

Just like her mother, stubborn to the end.

I held a private cremation, but a few of her friends showed up. I knew they were from the rebellion. I was going to ask them to leave, but they filed in quietly, holding their own grief. We stood together, saying our goodbyes.

Afterwards, I walked to a nearby park. There was a brisk wind, greenery, sounds of birds, but it was all holograms and metal. So many parts of nature were dying or gone. For the first time in a long time, I thought of Amaya. And I knew, deep in my core, this wasn't what she envisioned when she said we should fix nature.

A young man from Jayde's group approached me. He sat next to me on the park bench. His features were dark, his eyes had a familiarity to them. Like Amaya's. Or maybe I was imagining it.

"She was working with the movement," he said.

"I know."

"Not Jayde. Amaya." I looked at him but didn't say anything. "When she figured out how to replicate the flower, she was going to give it to us. She wanted to put it in the hands of the people." He waited for a response but I stared out into the park. "It was always meant to be for healing and easing pain. You turned it into something else."

"You know nothing, you're a child."

He scoffed, "We have been passing down stories through each generation. We never died. Just like you." He stood up, ready to leave. "Your company killed her; they knew she had figured out how to replicate the flower."

"That's not true." It couldn't be true. It was a trick to confuse me, to exploit my grief. I knew because this is what I did to them.

"They never wanted it to be mass-produced, so they got rid of her."

"They needed her."

"Only until they understood her research, after that, she was disposable. Just like the bugs in your body." He walked away and joined his group.

My hands were clenched tight and I couldn't move. I looked around and the park had emptied out. I walked back to the crematorium and got the urn with Jayde in it. When I got to my car, it started up on its own. The car door opened, slapping my hand, and the urn dropped. The ashes fell to the ground, flying everywhere. I got on my knees and gathered what I could but bits had fallen through a grate leading to the underground roadways. I put my head down and for the first time that I could remember, I cried.

The bugs had given me life, and the bugs had taken life away from me.

I stood up and leaned against the car, barely able to catch my breath. I didn't want a life that didn't have Jayde in the world. I needed to join her, even if it meant meeting her in emptiness. And I hoped that maybe Amaya would be there too.

"I'm coming," I said.

* * *

This story first appeared in the After Dinner Conversation—October 2021 issue.

Discussion Questions

1. Do you agree with the statement "...science for the greater good means editing genes to improve humanity" or should science not attempt to improve humanity through gene editing?

2. Assuming the "bugs" could never be produced at scale, how should they be distributed to the public? Should they go to the highest bidder, go to the most needy, or distributed in some other way? Should the age of the person be a factor, that is to say, should a very old person with a terminal disease be given the "bugs?"

3. Isn't it reasonable that medical investors would want to maximize the profits from their research investments? Is it wrong that individual investors fund research the government is unable, or unwilling, to invest in?

4. What do you think would happen, how do you think it would be handled, if a company actually invented a medicine that could stop the aging process? How should it work in a just society? Why can't it work that way?

5. Is it appropriate for companies and/or governments to use (*or withhold*) access to medicine to encourage good behavior and improve global stability?

* * *

S o w

Joseph Bodie

* * *

Pilot's Log
12 March 2130
Days to Deployment: 5

Infinity is beautiful. If you've never seen it, it would be hard for me to describe the breathtaking wonder of an endless void. Some might find the solitude disquieting, but I have come to take comfort in the isolation.

It gives me time to think.

They told me this mission would be simple. Long and mentally and physically taxing, but simple in its directives:

- Locate Planet X1506-78.
- Locate fertile terrain.
- Deploy and dust terrain with panspermia capsules.
  Simple.

I know what's riding on this mission, what's at stake. I feel the weight of hopes millions and millions of light-years away. Physically and mentally taxing. But, for me, I have come to see this mission as morally taxing as well.

Do we deserve to preserve our species? What right do we have to disrupt the natural evolution of an alien planet? Is life sacred or profane?

I do not have the answers to these questions yet.

* * *

Pilot's Log
13 March 2130
Days to Deployment: 4

I spoke with my wife today. It's just a room now, I told her. It's time, I told her. You need to do this, it's healthy, I told her.

It's easy for me to say that. I'm not the one who has to remove the crib, the toys, the pictures on the wall. I'm not the one that will have to paint over all of those animals and their bright smiles and frolicking feet.

It's just a room now. Walls and a window and a floor and a ceiling. It's just a room as sterile and inhuman and indifferent as the white-walled hospital room with its machines and their beeps and hums and numbers on screens signifying a decline.

It's just a room now. Just like it was just a body in the end. A tiny 14-month-old body. It wasn't even a body. It was a host. It was a tiny 14-month-old cancer host.

It's just a room. It's just a body. It's just a host.

* * *

Pilot's Log
14 March 2130
Days to Deployment: 3

Is it better to have never been born at all? Given the unpredictable nature of life, given all of the possibilities for pain and pleasure, given the uncertainty of the ratio of pain to pleasure, given the question of the duration of the pain, of the pleasure, of the act of being alive itself, is it a gamble worth taking?

Thought experiment: I come to you with a proposition to join a game. If you choose not to play the game, you lose nothing. Everything stays the same.

However, if you choose to join the game, there is no guarantee as to how long you will play the game, how much pain or pleasure will come your way, and, most importantly, you have very limited agency in this game, your will is imposed upon by outside forces and is therefore not free.

Would you play?

* * *

Pilot's Log
16 March 2130
Days to Deployment: 1

Hope is a strange concept, a strange bedfellow, a savage lover. The concept itself has become a little absurd and irrational and naive to me. What good is it to invest in something that's wholly beyond your control?

Why has an entire planet of people placed their hope on me, on this mission, on these panspermia capsules?

To continue the human race? But what good does that do for them? They're dead anyway. Is there really any comfort or consolation in the notion that our species will live on this foreign planet?

And do we deserve to? After what we've done on and to ours? On and to our own species? On and to every other species that we claimed dominion over?

And what about these capsules? Do they even want to start the long and arduous process of evolution to become something so staggeringly inconsistent as us?

So loving and hateful and compassionate and indifferent and charitable and greedy and peaceful and murderous and on and on and on and on.

Do they even want to play the game?

* * *

Pilot's Log
17 March 2130
Deployment Day

This will be my last entry. I have made a decision, a choice, a commitment. Or I feel that it has been imposed upon me, so maybe I am not to blame for the consequences.

For posterity, in case this recording is ever transmitted: I feel that the moral course of action here is to self-destruct.

This will be a beginning just as violent and fiery and random as the beginning of all things.

There will still be a chance for some of the capsules to survive and fertilize the terrain.

Those that fight to live will have made their choice. They will play the game, for better or worse or whatever.

Who will survive and what will become of them?

* * *

This story first appeared in the After Dinner Conversation—June 2022 issue.

Discussion Questions

1. If you were the pilot in the story, would you drop the panspermia capsules on the planet, ending the potential natural evolution of the planet and seeding it to evolve your own species in the distant future?

2. To what degree would life have to already exist on the planet, for you to refuse to seed it with the panspermia capsules? What if the planet had a variety of thriving, but non-sentient, life already?

3. Does a species have the absolute right to continue its existence at the expense of others?

4. The pilot discusses life as a choice; "if you choose not to play the game, you lose nothing. Everything stays the same," but if you play, the game lasts an indefinite amount of time, and may be full of horrible pains or pleasure. In short, if given the choice prior to birth, would you choose to be born?

5. Given that the entire species has put their faith in the pilot to perform this task, and he agreed to perform this duty, does he have the right to change his mind on deployment day?

* * *

Two-Percenters

CJ Erick

* * *

Reginah stared at the crystal vial her friend Twylea had laid on her desk. A gentle light bloomed within the desk's frosty surface, illuminating the liquid sealed in the vial in shades of lavender.

"Go on," she prompted. Twylea could be annoyingly slow in disclosing useful context.

Reginah's friend, like all Socials, was divine-like in beauty, carved from alabaster and gold. Every pose, tiniest movement, or inflection in her voice was precisely tuned to thrill and disarm the observer. Even knowing this, Reginah often fell under her friend's spell. And today Twylea bore a gift.

"Imagine if you will," Twylea said, in the purr of a femme fatale, "a world where everyone could be a Two-Percenter."

Twylea was also intentionally vague, which she knew was frustrating for Rationals like Reginah. And she knew Reginah hated the commoners' label for her kind. It demeaned the Gifted's genetic superiority.

"That's been studied by hundreds of researchers," Reginah said. "The physiological and genetic inhibitions for those in the general population have never been successfully overcome. At least ten million commoners have died or been disfigured attempting it." She purposefully ignored the pretty ornament. "The council sponsors continue the research, but the consensus is it will never be done. Discussing it further is pointless fantasy."

Even for a "Two-Percenter," a genetically enhanced humanoid, Twylea was a stunning wonder, with enhancements focused on outward beauty, voice, posture, emotional expression. The perfect host, actor, debate panelist, politician. Inches taller than Reginah at nearly two full meters, body fit and toned with little or no work and built along Vitruvian mathematical proportions; flawless skin and golden hair framing her perfect heart-shaped face; eyes the color of the vial's lavender liquid, the color of wisdom, royalty, and first love; lips and cheeks and ears mathematically perfect; chameleon skin tone adapting to ambient light, mood, and purpose. Cleopatra or Helen or Aphrodite would pale in comparison.

Twylea's pianist's fingers tipped across the desk, and the inner light from the desk's surface sparkled from her golden nails. Her fingers stopped inches away and retreated. "Humor me for a minute." Reginah found she could do nothing else. "How many of us are there?"

"Here in the North American Region? Two per million. About one thousand. Worldwide—twenty thousand."

"How would you describe our influence?"

Reginah shook herself to clear her head. "Your Socratic

method is annoying. Get to the point." But Twylea just smiled. "Fine, I'll play."

Twylea's eyes twinkled. "Of course you will."

"Influence? We've been the driving force behind nearly every recent advancement—science, mathematics, physics, art... politics." She nodded toward Twylea as she spoke the last.

"For how long?"

"You know this, since 2045, when Orinheim and Hatomi perfected their recombinant techniques."

"And how far have we come in the last fifty years as a species?"

"Since the first hundred were identified and enhanced, trifold acceleration. Even our best statisticians struggle to define the rate of advancement. We continue to surpass the models."

Twylea smiled in approval, but it seemed bloodless, now that Reginah had withdrawn from her spell. Even her Social persona could not hide her inner tension from Reginah's Rational inspection.

"Yes. So imagine where we could go if all people could undergo the enhancements and not just the lucky few. Anything would be possible, perhaps even a final, complete understanding of the universe."

"Or total chaos, reminiscent of the Dark Ages. In the current structure, we lead progress, commerce, governance, albeit through shadow influence. There is no war, no poverty, little disease and that cured in weeks rather than years. The commoners recognize our superiority, if reminded gently on occasion, and we maintain order. But make us all relatively equal again—it could all break down. Or become obsolete. We just don't know."

Reginah cursed her friend silently, for wasting her time speculating worthless scenarios. It distracted from the work; twisted her mind in knots. "Either way, it would be 'Utopia,' in the Greek origins of the word—'No place.'—because it's never going to happen."

Twylea had let her disarming smile fall, something she seldom did. She bit her lip, something she never did.

"Do you think our privilege is fair?"

Reginah felt her friend's tension spread to her own thoughts. Why would Twylea push this question to her, a Rational? She wanted a Judicial, or a Sophist. Gratefully, she let Reginah off the hook and answered her own question.

"I don't," said Twylea. "For thousands of years, people have dreamed of gods coming from the sky to guide them, or feared others coming to make them pets."

"I know where you're going. We are not pet masters. Or puppeteers."

"We feed them. We keep water in their bowls, and even develop better ways to scoop their waste. And by not working to repair this imbalance, we sentence them to staying in their yards."

"At best, we are driving the new awakening. At worst, they live in pretty nice yards."

Twylea's smile didn't return, but her eyes turned their full mesmerizing power on Reginah. She pushed the vial inches forward with a finger so well shaped it resembled a ballet dancer's leg.

Reginah asked, "Is this a new deodorant for the yards?"

"You're very snide for a Rational. No, darling, this is the magic potion that turns all the pets into gods."

Twylea paused, expecting Reginah to provide the echo. "How?"

"Orinheim. He gave it to me before he... died." Dr. Benjamin Orinheim was the esteemed Rational presiding over the Bureau of Genetic Development, the agency through which all enhancements were orchestrated. Even among the Gifted, his name was spoken in hushed tones. *A god among gods*, she thought, then crushed it immediately. He'd died months earlier in a rare lab accident while repairing one of his gene-painting machines.

"Why did he spend his precious research time working on this problem?"

"Introspection. Regret, I think."

"Why did he give it to you?"

"He trusted me. I was selected to be one of his consorts."

"That bastard."

"No, I applied. This was Orinheim, Reginah. It made no sense for him to spend time pursuing relationships. But he still had personal needs."

"Maybe he should have 'enhanced' those away. And I'm not buying the regret explanation. He didn't create the rules that favor us. Why should he feel guilty to be Gifted?"

Twylea settled back into the formless ergo lounge, suddenly looking very human and very tired, like a five-a.m. harlot.

"I said regret, not guilt. He asked me to run an underground team to gather reports on the long-term effects of the growing class divide. Our findings were not encouraging."

"He carried on research without Institute sanction?"

Twylea's eyes twinkled again. "You would be surprised by

what influence can accomplish, even in Valhalla. What Orinheim wanted, he pursued."

It was Reginah's turn to sit back and feel tired. There was something very odd and yet suspiciously familiar about Twylea bringing the token and its story to her.

Twylea went on. "The edges are already starting to fray. The latest executive reports show more crime in nearly every district. Even violent crime, for the first time in 25 years, despite nearly universal surveillance and rapid response. Anti-government protests are growing in all seven continental regions. Psychosis, depression, suicide, all on the rise. And all of this supports our findings that things are not going well."

"And Dr. O's response was to make us all equal again, introducing a new age of unrestrained materialism, war, and class stratification beyond anything our best models can predict."

"Possibly. But no pets. No yards. No genetic lottery. No technological injustice."

"Just all the other really fine types of injustice. So why bring this to me? You have 'the cure.' Dr. O and his disciples believed this is the right thing to do. Why not release it to the world? Bring the New Age. Be heroes."

"His death wasn't an accident." Twylea's jaw was set, and her eyes drawn down, like Athena after she'd wet herself. "He couldn't live with himself not using it."

Reginah decided to wait her out this time, as long as it took. Meanwhile, part of her mind processed everything her friend had offered. The neural communications implant in her cortex accessed the Institute's Date and Records Library, and she reviewed the studies Twylea had referenced. Searching for an academic dagger, Reginah found none, no inconsistencies in Twylea's story. Of course, the foundation of her revelation, the secret studies and production of the contents of the vial, couldn't be corroborated, nor could she find any mention or rumor of them. So, none of it could be debunked.

Twylea sat forward again, eyeing the vial. "It adds a peptide sequence on three different chromosomes that simulate the family of genes that allow us to undergo enhancement therapy. Within weeks, most commoners can begin the enhancement treatments."

Reginah zoomed her eyes in, searching for telltales of molecular magic suspended in the liquid. But the genetic machinery, if it was there as Twylea said, was too elusory for even her enhanced vision. She shifted her spectrum further into the UV range, and the vial seemed to flare with neon fire. But it held its secrets, just colored liquid rocking in the faceted glass.

"So Dr. O solved the problem that a thousand studies couldn't."

"Yes." That, simply.

"The proof?"

"Thomas Belton."

"The late bloomer? I thought his parents raised him in a Regressive sect, and he was discovered late."

Belton had emerged in his mid-thirties, long after most Gifted were placed in the program. He had advanced quickly, now a Commercist, leading one of the three North American regional banks in Sacramento. Like most of the Gifted, Reginah had been identified at the age of seven during standardized testing, and her most suitable specialty gleaned over the next two years.

Twylea shook her head, a negative gesture that had crushed men's hearts.

"He was born a commoner. He applied for the research study, and Dr. Orinheim chose him for his age and demographic, and because his sect ties provided the perfect explanation. The transition took two years. There were others, many successful, but Dr. Belton the most so."

"So why hasn't this crossed over from the subjects to others?"

"The gene splicing is stable, and needs a vector." She nodded at the vial, but seemed to avoid touching it. "Dr. Orinheim chose a rhinovirus. The recipient develops a case of the sniffles, no more." She eyed the vial now with something like unhappiness. "And then they join us."

Reginah felt a safety valve about to pop, threatening to blow her annoyance all over the room.

"You're looking at that thing like it's a poisonous snake and not the healing elixir for all humanity's woes. There's a downside, obviously. Spill it, or stop wasting my time."

Twylea's frown deepened, and Reginah had to fight the urge to hug her. Her friend's voice dropped like a funeral recitation.

"It changes us also." And that, simply.

Reginah stifled a laugh. She'd at last deduced the real intention of this meeting. Twylea was conducting a psychology experiment, and Reginah was the subject.

"So I'm guessing we don't become double-gifted."

"No. At best, our enhancements are rejected over time, and we become... common, as you would say. Worse— debilitating handicaps. Worst—grotesque disfiguration and painful death." Her eyes swung up to meet Reginah's, and oh the act was excellent, award-worthy. A single tear gathered in Twylea's azure sea of an eye. "Socials suffer the most."

"How do you know this?"

"Dr. Orinheim modeled it, tried to eliminate the rejection. There were trials..." The tear she'd been nurturing slid down her cheek, like a fake glass pearl.

"Why me?" On the surface, her question meant why give Reginah the vial, but beneath that, why choose her for the study? Even as she thought this, a bristling pang of doubt pricked her mind. Damn Twylea and her agenda. Even Reginah's powers of logic and rationale couldn't protect her from the psychological hooks.

"Who else but a Rational, and who else among them but someone I can trust? Please don't hate me. I can't let it loose. I can't let it... I just can't. My niece, Freesia, a Social like me. I know it's the right thing—for the most people, for the future of our species—but I can't do this to MY people." She slumped, seemed to shrink into the body of a young girl, the person she had been before genetic magic had metamorphosed her into a goddess. "Please don't hate me."

As suddenly as a light going out, she rose and left the office. Left behind was the MacGuffin, the vial of colored liquid possessing incredible power. Or none.

After Twylea's after-image faded in Reginah's mind, she settled back in her chair, pushed herself down into a meditative state, and spoke the word that would trigger her mind into a deep trance.

"Spinneret."

Her mental processes divided into isolated silos. Her

persona, formerly called the "ego," stood aside much like a spectator at a sporting event, and she observed her logic center dissecting the inputs from Twylea's visit. She evaluated each of Twylea's assertions independently, categorized and filed them, and assigned multi-variable Monte Carlo probability curves to each. She then modeled a spectrum of systems, manipulating the individual assertions in hierarchical indices of weighted average relevance. Her communication portal again accessed the Institute's library to review relevant information in the databases. After these models processed the data to a resolution of initial findings, she adjusted those conclusions by analyzing Twylea's behavior, mood choices, and emotional expression. The algorithms churned for what seemed like hours, but when the processes were complete, she rose from the trance to find that only six minutes had passed.

With a certainty of 93.6 percent, she concluded that she had in fact been enrolled in a psychological experiment, with a similar certainty that her reaction and response would affect her future opportunities and career track. If it was a test, the vial contained only colored water, and the correct response was to smash it on a crowded walkway to simulate releasing the virus.

The most interesting aspect was that if Twylea's assertions were true and the vial contained genetic transformation, then the correct response was the same. The benefit of the many superseded the penalties for the few.

She needed a walk anyway.

She scooped the vial into her tunic pocket, took the tube down to ground level, then pushed through the building's security field and onto the softwalk. The crush of commoners on the walk spread away from her, giving her more than ample personal space as she melded into their flow, some nodding or tipping their sloped hats, most avoiding eye contact. The Institute discouraged special treatment for the Gifted, either deferential or negative, but their efforts were largely unsuccessful. The Gifted would never fit into common society any more than she could step onto this softwalk without causing ripples.

Likely under surveillance, she moved with the tortoise-like flow along the walk, stifling her inclination to press through them. The city was served by several modes of aerial and subterranean public transit, bullet tubes and sky buses, and many private options. And yet the press of walking humanity never lessened, as if there was an informal prohibition against modernity. The influence of fringe anti-progressive cults couldn't account for it.

Judging from the lack of fitness of the people near her and avoiding her attention, most of them weren't walking for exercise. Her nose informed that hygiene was also not a priority even in the summer heat. She could smell their disease and age and injury and addiction, in an effluvial miasma that identified all the ills that still pervaded the species. The best efforts of fifty years of Gifted influence had not ended these infirmities. Twylea's reporting that the vision of "perfect society" was regressing was borne out by the studies, both those performed by her people, and those of the commoner scientists.

These people were in decline, even as the work of Dr. O's group pushed the capabilities of the Gifted higher. Their problems had devolved into a race against time, the work to save these people. The seriousness of the stakes was exactly why this psychological study she'd been drafted into was so genius.

Eek, how piteous it would be to devolve from Gifted to commoner. Or even worse, to be crippled, a deviant, grotesque being, sub-common. She stifled a shudder, and wished for a strong breeze to freshen the city air. Almost on cue, the whoosh of a bank of urban ventilators kicked on, and a cool breeze carried with it the fragrances of clean linen and endorphins.

Ahead, two city blocks through the adaptive building towers, the city center park rested, like an Eden of green abundance. The circular softwalk around it was always filled with people, a perfect place to make her show of busting the vial and releasing the harpies.

Before she reached the park, at the next crossroad, commoners clotted the softwalk, gawking at some disturbance on the parallel roadway. She approached and the crowd parted, letting her pass. She didn't possess the arresting beauty of a Social, but she was still physically enhanced to a degree, and an impressive figure with clear dark skin and thick tresses of raven hair that she wore pulled back and tied. When she reached the curbed edge of the road, she found a vehicle accident, a cargo van stopped, and the burly unshaven man she assumed to be the driver. He knelt at the front of the vehicle, blubbering like someone insane.

"I didn't see her, I swear. She jumped out like a blur, faster'n the brakes could react!"

The "she" he referred to was Twylea, lying on her back on the pavement, partially under the van's front tracks.

The driver jerked when he saw Reginah. "I tried to stop, mum! I was too damn slow." He waved his hairy hands in the air above Twylea's face, afraid to touch her, or check for vital signs. From where Reginah stood, she could see none of the telltale signatures of life—chest rising, pulse in her neck and wrist, movement in her irises. Reginah didn't need to touch her to know the Social was dead. Reginah's throat clamped tight, so she could barely swallow.

To those pressing in around her, she asked, "Anyone call this in?"

An older woman about a foot shorter than Reginah, with limp graying hair and a pre-cancerous growth on her sallow face, said, "Yes, mum. I've signaled the Corp, and they're comin'."

"Very good."

The others crowded tighter, violating Reginah's space, risking the wrath of her discomfort. Some twitched the micro-cameras in their fingertips, capturing the scene. The driver buried his face in his hands. "Why did she do that? Oh god, I'm soooo sorry!"

Reginah willed the Social to end this ruse and rise, but she remained still and dead, with blood leaking from her sculpted ears and the corners of her temptress lips, the lavender pool eyes blood-rimmed and clouding over. Reginah forced herself to look away and surveyed the crowd instead, most standing motionless and stunned. Several men and women stared at Twylea and fondled themselves, apparently overcome by her beauty, even in death. Reginah felt her disgust rising like vomit. She wanted to strike them.

A few in the crowd were not staring at the dead Social. To a person, they were leering at Reginah with a combination of hatred and lust.

The wail of the Corp response team insinuated itself into her senses. To the older woman, she instructed, "Stay here until they clear the scene. Make sure you impress to them that it was not the driver's fault."

Which it wasn't. The modern auto-braking systems were nearly perfect at preventing accidents, and also vehicular suicide. Unless the victim was extremely motivated and quick.

She gripped the vial tightly in the bottom of her tunic pocket, and then stepped into the street and kicked Twylea's body once, hard, in the ribs. She ignored the squeals and gasps of the onlookers and walked away, leaving the smell of them behind her. At least the fool driver was shocked out of his inane sobbing.

She melded back into the flowing mass on the softwalk, back in the direction of her office, away from the city center, away from the crowds.

A few steps from her building, an opalescent tower shaped like a piece from an elaborate board game held the escalator down to the first level of the Under-City, a cavern of shops and restaurants that evolved almost nightly to address the changing needs of the populace. She paused and let the flow of commoners pass her by, all of them giving her a wide berth, but glancing back in curiosity. Rationals did not pause; they acted with decisive correctness, as if their actions would change the course of the future.

She pulled the vial from her pocket and eyed it, and her logic center fed her the new probability that it was what Twylea had claimed, well over eighty percent. There were dozens of commoners taking the escalator downward. She could toss it here and walk away.

Instead, she flicked the end of the vial off with her thumb, exposing the contents to the air. She raised it slowly to her nose and inhaled deeply, smelling ethanol, amines, potassium salts, and proteins.

She pushed into the flow of people, smelling their infirmities again. As she descended, she tapped drops of the liquid onto the handrail, then at the bottom wafted the nearly empty bottle back and forth among the throng. A young mother with a bluebell hair scarf pushed a child carriage with year-old twins dressed in the horrifying colors of pink and baby blue. When the mother looked away at a direction sign, Reginah sprinkled drops of liquid over the children's heads. She abandoned the empty bottle in a trash de-constructor.

She walked among the shops then, finding what she needed, a small auto-pay store that was serving as an apothecary by day. It would transform into a social club for dinner or recreational drug use in the evening. When she entered, faces turned toward her, like the dishes of radio receivers. There was one worker or proprietor, a man of perhaps 50 years, with a clear bronze face and ebony hair too nice, enhanced in the lesser ways available to a commoner with good finances. Surprised and uncomfortable, he watched her as she searched among the aisles, until she found the place where deodorants were displayed. Across the aisle, feminine cosmetics were arranged in colorful rainbow displays intended to hook the users. When she stopped there, examining the products, the man approached.

"G'day, ma'am. Is there something I may... assist you with?"

She gestured toward the cosmetic display. Her fingers were long and straight and sublimely shaped, and her nails perfectly symmetrical, without a cuticle. They would not remain that way.

"I'm," she said. "I'm... going to need... some of these things."

* * *

This story first appeared in the After Dinner Conversation—March 2022 issue.

Discussion Questions

1. Was it ethical to enhance 2% of the population in the first place, if the entire population was not able to be enhanced?
2. Does the human race have a collective obligation to continue to improve our species? Does the human race have any collective obligation at all?
3. It is okay for those with enhancements to have greater influence over the course of the world? Should the smartest make the policy decisions for the world? Is there a group that should have a greater world influence? Is there a group that currently does?
4. According to the reading, enhancing the 98% will wreck the 2%. Would anyone in the 2% ever volunteer to give up their place of distinction? If you were in the 2%, would you?
5. It is ever ethical to take away from one person, to raise up another? What about our progressive tax system that taxes the rich at a higher rate to benefit those with less? Can you think of other "real world" examples that you agree or disagree with?

* * *

We Don't Do Faux

Gordon Sun

* * *

"你好, Fu 先生. Welcome back," Libby said, firmly shaking her customer's hand.

"Libby 小姐," Mr. Fu replied crisply, taking a seat in Libby's brightly lit, pastel-colored office. Two bald, grim-faced men wearing mirrored sunglasses took up positions by the doorway on either side, hands clasped behind their backs.

With his full head of jet-black hair and tan, elastic skin, the octogenarian Mr. Fu looked half his stated age, the culmination of a decades-long regimen of nanotech, genetic editing, and other routine medical maintenance made affordable by his enormous bank account. Coupled with an excellent diet and a vigorous, healthy lifestyle, the tuxedoed entrepreneur was the poster child for Phoenix Rejuvenative Sciences Center, Libby's employer.

"Mr. Fu, please confirm that you're here for cerebral regenerative nanotherapy," Libby said.

"是." Mr. Fu smiled. "It's time."

"Confirmed." Libby examined her monitors. "Four months, on the dot."

"Yes. Pre-paid in cash."

"Of course." Libby folded her hands on the desk, giving her most charming smile. "Now, you are aware that given your biological age, we recommend that the frequency of administration be increased to every three months once you enter your ninth decade. The dose will also need to be increased. Cellular damage accumulates faster as you age, Fenixir or no. Our nanobots are working against time to repair everything so you stay healthy and functional. They're miraculous, no doubt, but they don't confer immortality. Frailty becomes an issue—"

"Don't need to hear all the specs, Libby." The businessman nodded. "Just put it on the autopay."

"Certainly." Libby clicked a few buttons, and the PRSC had doubled their income stream from Mr. Fu. *Just like that*, she thought to herself. "It looks like the regimen's really working for you, Fu 先生," she continued, chuckling.

"It is, thanks to you and your team."

"Don't thank me. I'm neither the roboticists who developed the nanotech nor the engineers who refined it for human consumption."

"哎呀, take the credit. You don't know how much this means to me. Fenixir is well worth the cost."

"Do tell."

"Thanks to Fenixir, I literally doubled the length of my career, without the physical and cognitive declines that come with age and that in other times might have gotten a relic like me kicked to the curb twenty or twenty-five years ago. It gives the benefit of being able to think long term, very long term, beyond the day-to-day fluctuations of the markets. Returns multiplied. Fortunes were made, far, far bigger than what I've spent here."

Libby kept her smile on. "Good for you."

"Also, looking youthful and vigorous is an asset in today's world, no matter where you work." Mr. Fu laughed. "Libby 小姐, you are too young and pretty to understand. It's okay. Need experiences, good and bad, to grow."

"Hopefully more positive than negative." Libby adjusted the collar of her white office jumpsuit.

"True. Anyway, thank you for indulging an old man, even if I don't look it."

"Of course. Doctor Nimata will be personally overseeing your case, as usual." Libby's office door slid open. "Have a wonderful afternoon."

By the time the last of Libby's fifteen customers departed, a crescent moon hung in the clear nighttime sky. The Los Angeles skyline glowed with the lights of countless skyscrapers and endless rivers of traffic, saturating her office with a yellowish glow. Libby skimmed her emails, pausing briefly to read the memo announcing her third consecutive quarter atop the regional sales rankings. Finally, she began typing up all her client interaction notes for the day.

As she opened Mr. Fu's clinical records, her glasses vibrated from an incoming call. She tapped the right earpiece with her finger, and the face of a small girl in a white cotton gown appeared. "Hi, Mommy!"

"Anna!" Libby stood from her armchair and walked away from her desk. "Is everything okay?"

"Yeah, Mommy. They had to poke my arm again. The IV

fell out."

"Aw, sweetie. Are you okay?"

"I'm okay. They gave me ice cream."

Libby laughed. "That's good. Hey, I'm sorry I haven't come by yet today. Mommy had to work late again."

"It's okay, Mommy. I know I'll see you soon."

"Is your nurse there?"

"Yeah." There was a rustling sound, and the face of an older woman in light green scrubs appeared on Libby's lenses.

"Hello?" Libby asked.

"Hi there, Miss Wells. This is Joanna, Anna's nurse for today."

"Anything I need to know about?"

"Anna did fine today. We had to replace her IV, as you just heard, but she is eating well and staying hydrated. Her counts are still quite low, and her fever hasn't come down all the way yet, so she'll be with us for a little while yet."

Libby sighed. "I understand. How about the clinical trial? Any word from Doctor Siu?"

"He's still trying to get your case reviewed."

"Fine." Libby paused. "Please tell Anna I'll be there in an hour or so. I'm finishing up work."

"No problem. I'm on evening shift, so we'll probably see each other when you get here."

"Thanks."

"You're welcome. Take care." The call ended.

Libby returned to her seat and leaned back, frowning. The clinical trial enrollment process was going way too slowly. Anna already had surgery, radiotherapy, and chemotherapy four months ago, which slowed but didn't stop the glioblastoma multiforme creeping through her brain, though the treatments did manage to eat through all of Libby's savings. And even if Libby's little trooper got into the trial by some miracle, they all knew what was in store: more chemotherapy, more radiotherapy.

More suffering.

* * *

"Total package, then?" Libby asked.

"Yeah, baby!" the client responded with a desultory wave. Libby bit her tongue. "Brain and body regen, double dose. Plus, the detox module for the liver."

"I see." Libby hesitated for a moment. "Well, Mr. Gladstone, it's your decision of course. That said, there's no clinical benefit to doubling the recommended dose of Fenixir. The body simply eliminates the excess via urine and stool."

"Whatever. More's always better in my book." The young man smirked, smoothing his red silk tie. "Kinda funny that you're, like, trying to get me to spend *less* money."

Considering I'm half-commission with crappy benefits, yeah, it kind of goes against my revenue model. Too bad I have a conscience. "You need not worry about me. PRSC's concern is first and foremost for the safety of its clients. Second, exaggerating effectiveness sells our products short and only leads to long-term customer dissatisfaction and degradation of our reputation." Libby gave one of her patented knowing smiles. "In other words, our high-performance products speak for themselves."

"Yeah, that's why I'm here. Anything else?"

"My other question for you is regarding the hepatic detox module. Certainly, the surgical risk is low with our experts over in augmentation, but typically people request this particular bionic implant due to, ah, past health issues related to excessive, chronic consumption of alcohol and/or certain drugs. Your questionnaire indicated no such—"

"Look, Libby, it's real simple." Mr. Gladstone leaned forward, his mane of wavy brown hair falling over his forehead. "I run a fast-growing startup soc-tech company—maybe you've heard of it, it's—"

"I see it in my files, thanks," Libby replied, politely but firmly.

"Yeah, anyway, I've got to wine and dine investors, collaborators, that sort of thing, like all the time. Not gonna lie, there's partying too, lots of it. Sure, I'm not drinking every day, but I've got to be able to handle whatever the clients throw at me, like an entire bottle of bespoke bourbon or a whole night of drinking in some sushi bar. It's happened before." He grinned. "I mean, it's a big reason why I'm getting the body regen, also. I hear it's like an energy boost that lasts an entire damn year. And you know it's important to maintain stamina. Not just so I don't, like, fall asleep during boring meetings and crap, but also for more entertaining stuff. You know, like when I'm out with a bunch of wom—"

"I get the picture," said Libby, swallowing the bile surging in her throat. She pressed the button on her desk to open her office door. "Doctor Simmons will be handling your case, both the Fenixir and the liver implant. The clinic will reach out to you shortly to schedule the intake with him, as well as the required preoperative labs and studies. Thank you for choosing Phoenix Rejuvenative Sciences Center."

Dr. Ellen Nimata craned her head into Libby's office a

couple of minutes after Mr. Gladstone left. "How are things, Miss Wells?" she asked, her voice brisk.

"Fine. Just got a couple clients left to see."

"Our star product specialist, working hard as always. Your sales figures haven't gone unnoticed." The medical director of the Los Angeles branch stood in the doorway, as other staffers murmured their greetings and quickly passed by, heads lowered. "The director of augmentation just called me. This last guy, Chase Gladstone—how did you get him to buy the deluxe package, with the bionic add-on? It's usually a tough sell." Dr. Nimata tilted her head inquisitively.

"I didn't do anything, honestly. He requested it. Said it was for his job."

"And double the Fenixir dosage? That's an uncommon request."

"He was convinced it would help his...stamina."

"Of course. No problem. Anyway, twice the recommended dosage is ultimately harmless, if perhaps a little wasteful." Dr. Nimata shrugged dismissively. "How's your little daughter, by the way?"

"Anna's fine," Libby said quickly. Personal matters didn't belong in the workplace.

"Okay. Good to hear." The doctor nodded and turned away. Her voice carried down the hall as she walked off. "Don't stay too late."

"Sure, Doctor Nimata."

Later, on the way out the lobby of the building, Libby noticed that the brawny security guards, both of whom had been out of the office the past several days, were each sporting a new bionic left eye. Their irises glowed a bright blue as they scanned pedestrians and connected to the wireless security cams dotting the building.

Libby puzzled over how the two guards, hardly the highest-paid employees of PRSC, could afford million-dollar implants. It then occurred to her that the company probably *paid* for the procedures, considering them investments in their assets. She wondered how enthusiastic—or not—the guards were about it.

For a long, lingering moment, she toyed with the idea of pleading with her boss to cover nanotherapy for Anna. But finally, she put the thought aside. Anna wasn't an asset to the company.

* * *

Libby forced herself to return to the conversation. The couple that had just sat down in her office had *opinions*.

"Listen, honey," the heavyset woman was saying in a syrupy sweet voice, "we don't do faux. Bionic products don't last."

"Absolutely," her equally obese husband chimed in. "Genzen Technologies had to recall their entire line of bionic hearts because the pacemakers kept getting hacked. And that one company, I forgot the name—they had that contaminated batch of 3-D printer material. People *died*."

"So, yeah, that's why I'm here," the woman concluded. "I need Fenixir. For my pancreas."

"Pancreas?" Libby echoed.

"Yeah," the woman replied, fluttering her pudgy, heavily bejeweled hands. "Goddamn pancreatic cancer, like I was saying. Stage three. They say it's from the smoking and the drinking."

"And the diet," the man chuckled.

"Oh, *definitely* the diet," the woman said, snorting. "But, seriously, I'm never gonna be able to lay off the meat and potatoes. And the chardonnay. So, you've got it in stock, right?"

"Of course, Missus Smith," Libby replied slowly. "Every branch maintains a large, customizable pool. It's refreshed daily."

"Great," she said, loudly blowing her nose into a handkerchief she'd pulled out of a pocket.

Libby scanned her client's records. "Now, are you sure Fenixir is what you're looking for? Given your—lifestyle choices, you may need more frequent booster injections. In the interest of disclosure, these can add up. My colleagues over in augmentation can talk more about our bionic—"

"Honey, were you listening to a word I said?" Mrs. Smith snapped, folding the handkerchief and putting it back in her pocket.

"Don't try to upsell us, lady," Mr. Smith chimed in, fleshy jowls quivering. "We're small business owners. We know your tricks."

Libby sighed and started typing the Smiths' request into her workstation.

"You could be a little more enthusiastic," Mrs. Smith sniffed. "We could've gone to Doctor Gillespie in Beverly Hills for a designer pancreas, with add-ons and everything."

"Is my wife going to be able to get the injection today?" Mr. Smith demanded.

"Unfortunately, no," Libby replied. "You'll need to see one of our doctors first and go through our battery of tests. The nanobots need to be programmed and activated, based on your biochemistry, underlying target condition, and so on. The media gets it wrong a lot; it's not quite 'inject and forget.' There's nuance—"

"Are you serious?" Mrs. Smith cut in. The blotches on her pockmarked face grew a little redder. "We're paying top dollar, *top dollar*. Least you all could do is be a little quicker."

"The longer we wait, the more that damn cancer's gonna spread," her husband said curtly. "If this drags on too long, my wife's gonna look like Swiss cheese when the nanobots finish eating up all the disease. Don't want to have to rebuild her entire fucking body. I like it just the way it is."

"Oh, yeah, I bet you do," the woman leered, as her husband cackled.

Libby sighed again, fingers flying across the keyboard. "We'll do the best we can to accommodate your needs."

"Try to sound like you mean it, honey," Mrs. Smith replied, rolling her eyes.

Before she could open her mouth and say something she might regret, Libby's lenses reported an incoming call. She hit a few more buttons on her keyboard with finality. "Okay, you're set up with Doctor Hernandez. Please check out with our office manager, and she'll help you set up your follow-up visits. Thanks for choosing PRSC." Libby nodded her head at the door and pressed her right earpiece. "Hello?"

"Come on, Terry, let's go," Mrs. Smith said, glowering as she stood up. "The brat's apparently got more important clients." Libby ignored the couple huffily stomping out of her office, trying to hear the speaker.

"Libby Wells?" asked the voice.

"Yes, that's me," Libby replied hurriedly. "Sorry,

someone was just leaving my office."

"This is Meghan, Anna's nurse for today," the voice replied. "I wanted to let you know that Anna's been more sluggish than usual over the last couple of hours. Doctor Siu just saw her and is planning to transfer her to the ICU. He's also ordered a few tests. If you could—"

Libby barely heard the rest of the nurse's remarks as she bolted out of her office.

* * *

"So, not to be too pedantic, but data analytics requires both the space for the data and the processing power to crunch the numbers. The cerebral regen from Fenixir would keep my mind sharp, while having the BCI implanted would facilitate—" The speaker paused, a look of concern on his face. "—ah, miss, are you okay?"

Libby was exhausted, despite taking a cold shower at the hospital and drinking two tall cups of espresso. She didn't sleep at all the previous night, holding vigil as her daughter drifted in and out of a stupor. The ICU room contained more medical equipment than free space, the beeping monitors, robot arms, wires, and sensors swarming over Anna's small form like a watchful but intimidating electronic nanny. Even with eight years of medical sales experience under her belt and plenty of face time guiding patients through cutting-edge procedures at PRSC, Libby still wasn't used to being on the other side of the conversation.

"Miss?" the man asked again. "Libby?"

"Oh! Right." Libby shook her head. Her client's face was a bit blurry. "Mister Adelson, I apologize. There was...a family emergency last night." She blinked her scratchy, bloodshot eyes.

"I'm sorry to hear that. However, I do wish to move forward with the purchase, so is there anything you can do to—"

"Yes, of course." She reached for the cup of coffee on her desk, her hand trembling slightly. "Why don't I...why don't I transfer your case to my colleague next door? Natalie should be able to help you."

"Wait, that's not what I meant," Mr. Adelson said, a bit taken aback. "We can still work—"

"I think it's for the best, sir," Libby replied, trying to hide her relief as she sent her associate a quick message. "I want to make sure your experience with PRSC...is optimized. Natalie Womack is new to us, but capable." She entered a few more keystrokes and hit the Enter button. "If you turn right after leaving the room, her office is two doors down from mine, on the right-hand side. Can't miss it."

As the office door whirred open, her client stood up, nonplussed.

"Thank you for choosing PRSC for your therapeutic needs, sir." Libby smiled weakly as he left.

Libby knew her supervisor monitored client interactions like a hawk, so she fully expected Dr. Nimata to angrily burst through her door at any moment, demanding an explanation for the dump-off.

But the medical director never came by.

Maybe the doctor was busy with other things, she reasoned. Maybe Mr. Adelson didn't complain enough to warrant an intervention. Still, Libby felt only a minimal sense of respite, glancing at the four new consultations remaining on her docket.

Libby skipped lunch, struggling through the rest of her caseload. As soon as the last client left her room and the clock hit 17:30, she dimmed the lights and locked the door. Sliding open a desk drawer, Libby pulled out a small programmable chip drive, about the size of a dime, containing Anna's genetic information. The drive, no longer needed, had been given to her by a dejected Dr. Siu after his attempt to get Anna enrolled in the clinical trial was rebuffed.

Libby was initially upset, but she recovered quicker than even she would have thought possible. Maybe it was the inevitability of it all.

In truth, few options were left. She could watch her daughter die in pain...or she could intervene.

Libby stayed in her office for the next couple of hours, typing up reports and answering emails, watching the sun set behind the jagged skyline. Once the foot traffic in the hallway had quieted down, she ventured out. Her office badge dangling from a chain around her neck, she walked briskly to the elevators, pushing the UP button.

A few moments later, Libby entered the familiar laboratory, a vast repository for PRSC products taking up the entire floor. One wing of the floor was occupied by the "depot," where PRSC's nanobots were locally manufactured and programmed. She could see the watery solution through the faintly tinted glass wall: thin, grayish fluid stored in large vats, pluripotent like human stem cells. Large steel pipes pumped water and coolant around the tanks. Smaller vials and tubes packed in plastic racks on cabinet shelves contained activated Fenixir, a turbulent, smoky liquid churning with the purposeful activity of billions of nanites.

Libby slipped the badge off her neck. Twisting the chain absently around her hand, she stood in front of the depot, lost in thought.

* * *

Dr. Nimata appeared at Libby's office door before the first clients arrived for the day. "Libby, do you have a few minutes?" Her thin frame formed a scarecrow-like shadow in the doorway.

In the dim early morning light, Libby noticed for the first time faint bluish lines flickering under Dr. Nimata's temples. It seemed like many of PRSC's employees had undergone the aug knife. She wondered what other upgrades the medical director carried within her body. "Of course. Please come in."

The door slid closed behind Dr. Nimata as she entered and sat down in the guest chair. She straightened her crisp, long white lab coat. "You called in sick yesterday. Are you feeling better?"

"Yes, thanks. Had a really nasty headache. It was hard to think clearly."

"Hmm. You do have to take care of yourself, of course. I understand. It's tough having to balance a career while taking care of a child. Even taking one day off can be a big deal." Dr. Nimata watched as Libby sipped from a cup of espresso. "Anyway, just so you're aware, we're impressed with your portfolio of work. You've had a few interactions with clients the last week or so that perhaps had room for improvement, but all in all, very strong."

Libby nodded.

"How is she doing, by the way?" Dr. Nimata's tone was casual, but her eyes scrutinized Libby's face. Libby could not meet her gaze.

"Who?"

"Anna, your daughter."

"She's better."

"Oh, was she sick too?"

Libby hesitated. "She's been sick for a while now. I don't really talk about it."

"Sorry to hear that. But she has improved now, yes?"

"Yes, she has."

"That's good. What do you think happened?"

Libby was silent.

"Come on, Libby. You were caught on six different security cams even *before* you entered the depot—using your own badge, by the way." Dr. Nimata's smile was frosty. "You obviously knew you would be caught. At least now I know why you did it."

Libby finally looked up. "She was going to die," she said quietly. "Weeks, most likely. The other treatments were just a delaying tactic. She couldn't get into the clinical trial, and even if she did, it would have been more chemo and radiation. I know how effective Fenixir is, at least in adults—I've been selling it here for five years."

"So, you admit to stealing corporate property."

Libby took a deep breath. "No regrets, Doctor Nimata. It was worth it. I know how cheap Fenixir is to manufacture and how much profit margin we make off it." The words flowed easily from Libby's mouth now. "Of course, that high cost is why my lousy insurance policy won't cover it, and you think I can afford it on a saleswoman's salary, top performer or no? Here's my question: why didn't you stop me?"

"I admit you were quite brazen about it. That said, before PRSC pursued any definitive course of action, I wanted to gain insight into why our star performer decided to throw it all away. Clearly it had to be something important."

Libby raised her eyebrows. "It's what any mother would do for her daughter."

"I completely understand the rationale for your actions, of course. I *am* still a doctor, even though you probably think I don't act like one." Dr. Nimata harrumphed. "What would you do if you were us?"

"Fire me."

"You would want that, I'm sure." The medical director tutted. "I'm sure you'd find some bottom-feeder lawyer willing to amplify the optics of a multinational company firing a single mother of a sick child."

Libby sniffed. "Then I suppose I could resign on my own."

"Slightly better option, and we could invoke the NDA-NCC you signed upon hiring that would effectively keep you quiet and out of this field—for that matter, anywhere in pharma and biotech—for a very long time. Still, some of our longtime clients, ones like Mister Fu who are particularly fond of you, might ask questions as to why you suddenly left without explanation. Workforce gossip is another issue we'd have to manage. After all, you are the region's top sales performer. Obviously, discretion is in everyone's best interest." Dr. Nimata crossed her arms. "At the same time, our trust in you is severely damaged, and there's no way PRSC will tolerate theft."

"Okay, then why not spin this in a way that benefits everyone? Since Fenixir is only approved for adults, you authorized onetime use to help a dying child in an experimental capacity. Anna was the example, the proof of concept in the pediatric population. Sure, the hospital would have appreciated more involvement in the treatment process, but at the end of the day Anna got better very quickly and it cost them nothing, so they can't complain."

"You can make a sales pitch, that's for sure. Your top performance is no fluke." Dr. Nimata chuckled darkly as the lines on her temples glowed. "However, even though I acknowledge it could be a mutual win, it still lets you off the hook. If you're going to play these games with us, you're going to have real skin in the game moving forward. Fortunately, you've given me an idea, a way to help pay off your debt to us. A 'proof of concept,' if you will."

* * *

"I'll be honest, Miss Wells, I've already been to Intelid Pharma about my condition. Consider this a second opinion."

"Sure, Mister Hyung."

"Call me Albert. Anyway, I'm in the market for a new liver. I've got ALD—"

"ALD?"

"Alcoholic liver disease."

"Oh, right."

"None of my relatives are compatible, and I hear that the shortage of traditional donor livers means that given my alcohol use, I'm going to be at the bottom of the UNOS list." The sallow-faced man stared at Libby with yellowed eyes. "Intelid says they can clone part of my liver, grow it into a healthy new one within a few weeks. But I don't know..."

"What's your concern, Albert?"

"I'm no doc, but my liver is shot to hell. Wouldn't cloning it just carry over all the damage?"

Libby chose her words carefully. "It might, it might not. I'd have to refer you to one of our medical directors for explicit medical advice. However, I'll propose an alternative: our line of bionic livers."

"Tell me more."

"Here in the augmentation division, PRSC customizes and builds each device in-house, made to order. Because they are artificially constructed, we can install all sorts of upgrades that make it even more versatile than the original thing: for example, poison neutralization, alcohol detox. Your threshold for alcohol consumption without intoxication would increase to astronomical levels. You'd be unaffected by numerous toxic compounds in case of accidental ingestion or overdose."

"That does sound intriguing. What's your experience with this?"

"PRSC has been in the augmentation business for over ten years. Perhaps not as long as a couple of the other major players, but I can assure you that PRSC's results will exceed your expectations. Let me show you." Libby stood up and began to untuck her blouse from her pants.

"Um, Miss Wells, what are you doing—"

"Sorry. Bear with me for a moment." Libby flipped the hem of the blouse up. Several freshly healed linear scars of varying lengths crisscrossed her bare abdomen.

The client's jaw dropped. "Oh my—what happened?"

Libby lightly traced one of the scars with a finger. The incisions were painless, healing without difficulty. The PRSC surgical team was unquestionably good at what they did. "I underwent implantation of one of our very own customized livers right here at PRSC, with all the upgrades I just mentioned and more. Of course, there's a recovery period, so you can't return to work immediately. However, as you can see, I'm doing quite well. The plan is to be here for a very long time." She tucked her uniform in and sat down. "A compelling argument, wouldn't you say?"

"Indeed. Maybe we could talk about some of PRSC's other bionic enhancements if you have time today?"

"Of course."

Mr. Hyung nodded in satisfaction. "So, was it worth it?"

Libby thought of her daughter, recovering at home cancer-free, enjoying life, making plans for a far future, and smiled. "Yes. Without a doubt."

* * *

This story first appeared in the After Dinner Conversation—February 2022 issue.

Discussion Questions

1. Assuming no scarcity, should medical procedures be dependent on a client's ability to pay? Even if the procedure isn't difficult or scarce, should it be made available in a way (or price) that maximizes profits?

2. When medical resources are limited/scarce, what should be the criteria/process to determine patient prioritization; ability to pay, relative need, how the medical need came about?

3. Would you be more sympathetic to profit maximizing in the story if the profits went directly back into research for additional medical treatments rather than shareholder dividends?

4. What, if any, punishment should happen to Libby for stealing? Should "necessity" be a defense to criminal conviction?

5. What do you think the ending of the story means? Why did Libby have a bionic liver?

* * *

Pandora's Dreams

Peter Beaumont

* * *

Five years ago we opened Pandora's box. Blinded by hubris, we didn't foresee the problems that would arise. Only later did we realize our work would have such horrible implications, and as the story of Pandora goes, it's too late once the bad stuff gets out of the box. Now things are a mess and I guess we are to blame. You would be right to judge us harshly, and I won't hope for your forgiveness, but perhaps you might eventually understand how we got here and where we might end up if something isn't done.

I still remember the day well. It was early spring. A tang of vitality hung in the mild morning air as I climbed out of my car and walked slowly to the lab, weary from the late night and stuck in a loop of thinking I couldn't escape. Why wasn't it working? Where had we gone wrong? What had I missed?

We had been working late all week, sustained by a stubborn, almost desperate self-belief. We knew we were close. Close enough to believe the next day would be the breakthrough. Or the next. We just had to keep at it and ignore the poisonous doubt lurking in the long pauses between conversation; the doubt that it actually might not be possible to achieve.

None of us wanted to walk away from the years of work. From the years of sweet-talking potential investors and cajoling skittish board members. From the years of telling each other and anyone else who would listen that if we couldn't make the biggest advancement in neuroscience in decades, then no one could.

We had run the latest version of the program seven nights in a row without success. Each morning we had grimly accepted the disappointment and sent the volunteers on their way. Each morning our frustration accumulated like weeds choking a garden, and I wondered which of us might crack first under the pressure.

Then something changed.

On the eighth morning the result for two of the subjects was different. The quality was poor, and there was no sound, but irrefutably and quite remarkably we had finally succeeded in recording and playing back a human dream.

There was a reverent silence for five, ten seconds, then the room burst into life. People were shouting, laughing. Someone slapped my back. I stood rooted to the spot, eyes still focused on the wall-mounted screen in stunned disbelief. Someone called out to replay it, and as we watched again, the significance of what we had achieved began to sink in.

I still feel a flicker of the awe from that day. Like the small tremors that continue long after an earthquake has struck.

Looking back, I know we should have paused during

those first heady days to consider the implications of what we were doing, but if you can imagine the excitement we experienced that day then you might understand why we didn't. We had persevered and been rewarded, and were doubly determined to stay the course from there on in.

To say all the possible implications were unknowable is inexcusable, I know. Just as I know all we could think about on that day, and for many after, was the startling, beautiful things we could do with our discovery. And if we were honest – at least with ourselves – some of us were also imagining fame and glory. We were only human after all.

You won't be surprised to know that once we fixed the bugs in the system and moved to the full trial phase, the first participant was a rich entrepreneur. One of that infamous group rich enough to build private spacecraft and a boldness that could mesmerize millions with a grand vision of the future.

Some of the team weren't happy about blurring the boundaries between science and capitalism, but given our benefactor was prepared to donate a sizable portion of his wealth to the trial it was impossible to say no. And let's face it. Science doesn't happen unless someone pays the bills, and compared to the stifling bureaucracy of the university system we worked in, his proposition was beautiful in its simplicity. All we had to do was allow him to be the first to use it. Beyond that he wanted nothing, and in return he gave us more than enough money to make our dream project real. What reasonable person could refuse that?

So there we were. We had worked out how to record dreams and play them back. I was almost going to say play back at our leisure, but five years of viewing the confused, disturbing, even horrific creations of the unconscious mind has been as far from leisure as you could imagine.

The project was originally conceived with a noble intent. We had theorized that the roots of mental illness, trauma and certain cognitive disorders lay hidden somewhere within the deep, dark folds of the unconscious mind. Dreams were a manifestation of this little-understood function of the human brain, and we were confident that if we could capture and analyze them, we might be able to tease out the causes of these afflictions, and just possibly, find a cure.

There was so much we could have achieved, but – and I'm ashamed to say this now – we allowed commercial interests to override our therapeutic goal.

Once news got out that we could record and play back dreams, people clamored to get access to it. And those able to pay the hefty price were more than happy to do so.

Overnight, orbiting Earth as a space tourist dropped to number two on the must-do list of the mega-rich and would-be famous. After that there was, as they say, no holding back the tide.

With that, our research unit was transformed into a corporate entity, and in the eyes of some – ourselves included – we stopped being scientists and became salesmen. Soon the researchers and technicians were outnumbered by the marketers, lawyers, accountants and the quickly despised band of executives who cared only for profit and growth.

A year after that we made the next important breakthrough, improving the technology so that it could be housed in a portable unit and used by our clients at home. We had to install some seriously large computing hardware in our new facility to be able to handle all the incoming dream data, and then hire loads more technicians to keep it all running, but it's what the customers – and therefore the shareholders – wanted, so no one balked at it.

The units were clunky at first, and a little unreliable, but that was fixed in time. More problematic was some of the early client feedback. A number of people were confused and shocked by what they were confronted with, and a few couldn't handle it at all. We did our best to reassure them, sometimes cajoled them, and where necessary, directed them to a discreet counseling service to work through the more unpleasant stuff. The lawyers had also insisted we get all clients to sign an indemnity absolving us of any responsibility for harm should it occur, and a few clients had to be reminded of this as a last resort. Despite all this, enough clients continued on to tell their friends and social media followers about the miracle of their captured dreams – with perhaps some judicious self-editing in the telling – which fanned the flames of envy and drove enough demand on which to base a business.

Eventually, anybody prepared to pay the charges could sign up for a week, a month, even a year of recording, and have their dreams polished and sent back before the end of each day for them to view. It should have been a great success story. But then the problems began to emerge.

It didn't take long before people realized they could sell their dreams. Or worse, that recorded dreams could be stolen and sold on the black market for a good price if they were entertaining enough.

Humanity has always had a hankering to be entertained, and here was a new form just waiting to be exploited. Sexy, terrifying, disturbing, poignant, mystifying, thrilling: dreams offered it all, and there was always someone somewhere prepared to pay to watch it. More than one of our critics described our business as producing just another form of pornography.

Then came the more *entrepreneurial* activity. Someone worked out that here was a wonderful means by which to blackmail the rich and vulnerable. They would threaten to make public a stolen copy of a more *problematic* dream if the targeted victim failed to pay a significant sum of money. Needless to say, the willingness of victims to pay increased markedly after the blackmailers released the dream of one notable public figure who tried to call their bluff.

We couldn't work out how the dreams were being stolen. We tried beefing up system security, but to no avail. Much to my anger and disgust I eventually had to accept that at least one of our own staff was involved. It seemed that not only were the rich happy to pay for our unique service, but sometimes those wanting to be rich were prepared to break the rules to join them.

It's fair to say the clients weren't impressed. Most of them received sizable and discreet payments from the company for their trouble. All part of doing business, according to the company executives.

As troubling as this was, it was far from the worst of it.

The government took an interest in our system, seeing it as a potential tool in the fight against crime and terrorism. Why wait until someone is stupid enough to let slip their plans, or to act on them? Why not catch them in the act of dreaming about it and use it as preemptory evidence against them instead?

Now I've nothing against public safety, but using our

technology in this way leaves us in a difficult situation. Are we obliged to report any dreams that might be suggestive of criminal intent? What if poor old client X had watched a particularly violent film the night before, and then had a dream influenced by it? What if client Y had suffered an intense trauma and their unconscious mind played it over and over again in an attempt to make sense of it? Would these dreams be sufficient to warrant intervention by the authorities, and therefore require us to report them? And whose job would it be to try to interpret and justify the dreams as being a reliable indicator of criminality? Or for that matter, to explain how an unconscious desire will invariably lead to conscious action?

The libertarian lawyers and philosophers have had a field day with it so far. Dreams are private property they argue, and shouldn't be interfered with or used against someone, regardless of the circumstances. They decry the trampling of human rights and question the morality of this newfound omniscient justice.

And where might it end? There are rumors the government will soon mandate that everyone have a unit installed at home to record their dreams and transmit them to some government agency for monitoring. I'll leave it to your imagination as to what that might lead to next.

Perhaps I'm imagining the worst, but I'm not alone. There's a small but growing protest movement speaking out these days. Much of their effort is directed at the government, but not surprisingly, they have also taken aim at us. Online harassment of the company is now a daily occurrence, and I've read more than my fair share of nasty emails and social media posts directed at me.

They're mostly demanding the technology be banned,

claiming it's dangerous and that we don't know what we are doing. Worse are the suggestions that we are part of a government conspiracy which can only be fixed by violent revolutionary means.

Several of my colleagues left recently, spooked supposedly by the more unpleasant attacks. I heard one or two were offered considerable sums to work for dream recording outfits starting up in countries with less stringent regulatory controls.

So be it. I have no right to judge them. Others can.

The time of my own reckoning is now close.

Yesterday I dreamt I was standing in the vast processing vault beneath our lab that houses the row after row of computer servers. In the dream I walked over to a terminal, logged in, then hesitated as I looked around at the quietly humming machines that store a million dreams and more. I knew what I had to do, but what person wouldn't pause at the thought of destroying their own creation?

Then cold certainty took over and I entered the command, ignored the alert that came up, and re-entered it. A moment passed, and then it was done. The servers powered down and left me sitting in an eerily silent space. I felt a pang of sadness, followed by a growing sense of dread, then the dream ended.

That was yesterday morning.

Today I sit in my apartment under house arrest, awaiting the arrival of the authorities. No reason was given in the notification, but I know my dream must have been the cause.

I should have known my dreams would be monitored when I recorded them. I had found watching them a strangely cathartic experience after focusing intently on those of others. Naively, I overlooked the prospect of the company and the government being interested in them as well.

Now I wait to be judged by some government inquisitor, and, I suppose, by you in time.

I wonder what advice Oppenheimer would have for me if he were here today.

In moments of despondent clarity I have wondered if we were meant to fully know our dreams; whether we opened a door to the unconscious world that was never meant to be opened. Perhaps we should just accept the notion that dreams serve a useful purpose and leave it at that. To accept that there are some things that will and should remain unknowable. After all, do we really want to confront the proposition that part of our brain is working autonomously, almost like a separate mind of its own? Based on some of my own dreams it seems my unconscious mind is more than ready to cast harsh judgment on me for my role in this.

Enough for now. There's little hope for me, but perhaps it's not too late for someone else to act. For someone to not just protest against the sinister future we are hurtling towards, but to lead a movement to prevent it. For someone brave enough to try to do what Pandora could not; to put the evils of the world back inside the box.

* * *

This story first appeared in the After Dinner Conversation—February 2021 issue.

Discussion Questions

1. If you could buy, and watch, the dreams of others, would you do it? Why or why not?

2. Would you allow your own dreams to be recorded? Would you allow them to be sold, or watched by others? What do you think our dreams reveal?

3. If you could buy and watch (*or have*) a particular dream, what topics or stories would you want to try out?

4. Do you think people who have (*or want to buy*) violent or deviant dreams are (*or will become*) violent or deviant people? Do you think dreams should be used to provide cause for believing a future crime will take place?

5. Do you think there are areas of scientific research, like atomic bombs, viruses, human cloning, or dream recording, that should be banned from ever being researched?

* * *

Words Of the Ancients

T. Lucas Earle

* * *

"Praising what is lost
Makes the remembrance dear. Well, call him hither;
We are reconciled, and the first view shall kill
All repetition: let him not ask our pardon;
The nature of his great offence is dead,
And deeper than oblivion we do bury
The incensing relics of it."
-'illian Shakes'eare

* * *

Part I

Kessler dreamt of his world freezing in the void, silent and lifeless. He awoke in a strange mood that morning and climbed down from his house to watch the cattle sleep. They twitched and moaned in the half-light of dawn. It was comforting to him to know that even on this strange planet, everyone dreamed. Even the beasts.

A villager quietly emerged from the mist and approached

the sleeping cattle. He patted one of them until it awoke. He guided the creature out of the pen and gave Kessler a solemn nod as he walked it toward the slaughterhouse. The beast gazed at Kessler with dull eyes and did not look away until it disappeared into the mist. Kessler sighed and climbed back into his house. He couldn't bring himself to eat breakfast that morning.

As the sun rose and the village came to life, Kessler stayed in his room, poring over glyphs, trying to decipher the language of the Ancients, hoping to uncover the elusive past of this glorious planet. The hours slipped by, until Kessler received word from a colleague that he was needed at a new excavation located some distance from the village. He collected his tools and a few reference documents, then promptly jumped out the window.

High above the forest bed, Kessler free fell for a moment before unfolding his wings and gliding through the forest, deftly dodging trees and branches. He alternated between gliding through the canopy and leaping along the forest bed, until he reached his destination.

The trees abruptly gave way to a grassy clearing. It was midday and the sun had burned away the morning mist. He shielded his eyes and looked up. A massive ruin stood before him, a long towering block leaning to one side, covered in vines, gray and crumbling in the hot sun—an ancient behemoth being wrestled to the ground, strangled by the foliage.

Kessler approached the team of scientists congregated around the base of the monument. He recognized most of them from previous excavations: Hissun, the engineer; Ki'en, the archaeologist, accompanied by his team; and his friend and neighbor, Ti'ek, the resident xenobiologist, who noticed Kessler first and bobbed his head to greet him. Kessler bobbed back and approached the group. Ki'en's team busied themselves, setting up tents and unloading equipment from their vehicles. Ti'ek lifted his tail, affectionately swatting Kessler's side as Kessler inspected the building closely. It was so weatherworn there was very little chance any glyphs were left intact on the structure. But Ti'ek seemed quite excited as he led Kessler into the ruins.

They approached a long descending shaft, half bouncing, half gliding down it until they reached the bottom. This was the largest ruin Kessler had ever seen.

They crawled through the tunnels dug by Ki'en and his team before emerging into a chamber bursting with energy and motion. The commotion seemed to be focused around the far wall of the chamber, where there stood a strange blue and white metal panel flush with the chamber wall, edged with glowing fluorescent strips.

Kessler had no idea what the object was, but he gathered it was something important. Ki'en explained that the panel was a door. And, because the hatch was completely sealed, Ki'en speculated the chamber beyond was most likely airtight, perfectly preserved. Ki'en's team had found a geothermal power generator below the cavern. Whoever made this room had wanted it to stand the difficult test of time. Kessler approached the door with reverence. He hoped there would be some intact glyphs preserved within the chamber.

Sessek, the engineer, was working with his team on severing the door's power supply in order to turn off the magnetic lock. Neither Ti'ek nor Kessler could contribute much to the procedure, so they crouched in the corner and attempted to contain their excitement.

Whatever lay behind this door had been waiting a dozen lifetimes to be found.

The panel slid into the wall, releasing a powerful gust of frigid air and bathing the cavern in a majestic white light. The group squinted into the chamber. They approached the door, carefully stepping into the room beyond. It was alive with mechanical equipment, blinking and pulsing. Its technology, advanced—its purpose, unknown.

They proceeded through the sterile white chamber, wingtips twitching nervously, tails raised and alert. No one spoke.

Through a side door, Kessler found a long room. Blocks of varying color were lined up in horizontal compartments along the wall. Kessler examined one cautiously, running his hands along its smooth surface. It was covered in unfamiliar glyphs. The object was topped with a hard flap. He pulled it back and beneath it were thousands of glyphs on thin layers of parchment. The awe nearly toppled him. Each and every block on the wall was filled with glyphs. Each one was packed with knowledge, bursting with hidden histories. Ti'ek stood next to him, occasionally clicking, as Kessler inspected each layer of thin parchment. Ti'ek asked what the glyphs meant. Kessler told him he had no idea.

Then Hissun's hand was on Kessler's shoulder, and he was being led to the entrance of another room where the engineers and architects were huddled, staring at rows of white pods.

At first, no one spoke. But every one of them knew what these pods were. The Ri'ik had slept in them for centuries as they sailed through the stars from their old, dying world to this vital new one. These were hibernation pods.

There could be no doubt these pods were built by the Ancients. And inside each pod was a creature, they presumed an Ancient, with the answers to a thousand questions.

Hissun, Sessek, and Ti'ek spent the remaining daylight hours and many of the sunless ones examining the technological differences between these pods and the Ri'ik's own. They began the cycling down process slowly with just one pod, picked at random, so as to safely awaken its inhabitant. Most of the team slept in the cavern, where they could set up heating units without worrying about damaging the find.

Kessler would not be separated from his work, so he slept in the hall of documents, wrapped in layers of heated blankets. He had spent so much of his life digging through the faded remnants of an ancient language, and yet, surrounded by millions of glyphs, he felt suddenly out of his depth. What would these glyphs sound like, spoken aloud? Would he even be able to hear the sounds? Perhaps the Ancients communicated with frequencies the Ri'ik could not perceive. Kessler's mind squirmed under the enormity of it all. He fell asleep with the irrational hope that the glyphs would somehow leak out from their bindings in the night and permeate his dreams, filling his mind with the wisdom of days long past.

The next morning, he immediately began poring over the documents. He couldn't decipher the symbols yet, but they were familiar in their general design, if not pattern. He constantly referred to his notes, matching each glyph with the few intact glyphs from other finds. It was Ti'ek's chirp that finally broke his concentration. He was crouched at the doorway, explaining that the awakening process was starting. Kessler leapt up, still clutching the document he had been examining.

Kessler watched, transfixed, as Hissun and Ti'ek slowly opened a pod. Strands of a gooey substance spilled out as the pod was pulled apart, leaving the creature within lying in a puddle at its base. The ancient monitoring equipment, as well as the Ri'ik's, hummed, telling everyone that the creature was alive.

As the last of the viscous substance ebbed away, a silence fell upon them.

Of all the theories Kessler and his colleagues had debated about the Ancient Ones, this was the one they had never entertained.

It was a cow.

One of the scientists, an engineer, actually wagged his tail.

Kessler saw the humor. That was, until the creature began to howl. It was a horrible, ear-splitting sonic explosion. And while disorientation was not unexpected, given the recent awakening of the animal, it was still rather alarming.

Quickly, Ti'ek and another biologist approached the animal with sedatives. The creature, though still sluggish, was surprisingly strong and managed to ram the other scientist, sending him tumbling into the far wall. But Ti'ek's syringe found a home in the beast's back, dropping it to the floor. The whole group of scientists pushed in while Ti'ek made sure it was not injured as it lay before them, breathing shallowly. It was not unconscious, only weakened.

It was a female, but it was bigger than the other cows. Its face was longer, and its eyes were larger, brighter, shockingly aware, and terrified. And it was making noises—noises unlike any they had ever heard a cow make. Ti'ek prepared more sedatives while Kessler listened to the incapacitated beast. The sounds it made involved a motion with its lips that Kessler had never seen before. Ti'ek swooped in with another syringe and crouched by the beast, but before he could level the syringe, Kessler's tail landed heavily across Ti'ek's chest. Kessler's wings spread protectively over the cow, and he screeched for his colleagues to stop. They retreated instantly, and looked on as he dropped to all fours and looked into the beast's eyes.

It was speaking.

The other scientists fell silent and listened to the creature. It was undeniable. The sounds had repeating patterns. It wasn't mewling, or whimpering, like the other cattle. It was speaking. But how could a cow speak? They had been dwelling alongside the beasts for decades now, and the creatures showed a pronounced lack of communicative or even cognitive skills.

Yet there she lay, speaking, pleading with them. Then, without warning, she stopped and looked directly at Kessler, who was still clutching the ancient document to his chest.

The two of them stared at each other for a moment before Kessler, remembering his training, placed his hand on his head. "Kessler," he said, simply.

The creature paused. Then it placed a pale paw on its upper torso and uttered a single word.

"Human."

* * *

Kessler sat across from the cow and watched as she inspected the glyphs on the hibernation pods.

She was refined, delicate even, for such a large and peculiarly proportioned animal. She opened a cubby and took out fabrics, which she wrapped around herself. She glanced at Kessler periodically as she went about investigating the pods.

Cows couldn't understand the simplest tools. It was odd—even humorous—watching one operating advanced machinery.

Kessler had persuaded the scientists to allow him to spend some time alone with the beast, to try to communicate without the distraction of the others. So far, the plan seemed to be working. She spoke often; although Kessler couldn't understand what she was trying to communicate. He tried speaking back, but she understood nothing. Kessler tried pointing at objects in the room and saying their names, but she didn't respond. So, instead, he opened his bag, where he had stored the document he had been studying earlier, and presented it to her.

She looked at it for a long moment. Then she opened it and sat down on the floor. As she examined the glyphs, she wiped moisture from her eyes, and her breathing became quite labored.

Kessler cautiously approached her. She did not react. He crawled next to her and looked at the parchment she was inspecting. She lifted the thin sheet and moved it to the left. He observed her eye movements. She was clearly reading the glyphs from left to right. Finally, Kessler worked up the courage to point, first at one glyph, then another, and another. She looked at him and he at her, his thin finger tapping the parchment. Then she spoke.

"Words," she said.

What a delightful sound she made. A bilabial! But of course she could, with prehensile lips. Kessler clicked with excitement.

Kessler was overjoyed to discover that the symbols the Ancients used were not glyphs at all, but phonemes. Each symbol did not represent a word but instead a single meaningful sound. It made her language simple to write. All he had to do was learn all the corresponding sounds, which was easy enough once he found replacements for all the bilabials.

He had finally figured out the tenses—the language actually had a means of conveying a future hypothetical situation that did not yet exist! The sophistication!—when he, quite surprisingly, blacked out. It was in mid-sentence, and it was only for a brief moment, but in no time at all he was lying in Sara's powerful arms. He shook his head and tried to stand up, but the room seemed to bend and wobble. Sara made frantic sounds.

"What's wrong?" she said.

"I hath not... eaten." His head ached. "Need thood."

"Food," she said.

Kessler nodded.

Kessler stood, Sara hovering over him in case he fell again. He tried not to make eye contact as he crept on all fours to the door. He tapped on the metal hatch a few times until it opened.

Under the warm rays of sunlight, a bright-eyed young villager brought him food. The young attendant hummed pleasantly as she laid out an assortment of foods. Once she was done arranging the food in the proper ceremonial manner, the villager watched Kessler expectantly, waiting politely for him to eat.

Kessler stared at the thin gray strips in the center of the platter.

* * *

Ti'ek and the other biologists came in daily to examine Sara. They found that she was, for the most part, biologically identical to the beasts they ate. The differences were minute enough to be caused by simple mutation—an extra chromosome.

* * *

"Let hin not ask our 'ardon."

They read together, as they had done the days prior. Kessler had quickly unpacked the syntax of the language and was in the process of devouring its majestic contexts.

"The nature oth his great othence is dead," he went on, "and dee'er than..."

"Oblivion," she said.

"Odlithian," he echoed, poorly. "O'at does it nean?"

"Oblivion? Let me think..." Kessler waited eagerly for the new concept. "It's where things go when they are lost forever."

Kessler stared at the word. Thoughts of his freezing homeworld came to mind.

A sharp rasping sound made him raise his head. Sara coughed once again, then she began to wheeze and clutch her chest. Kessler leapt to his feet, but, just as he was about to ask what was wrong, she collapsed. Kessler shouted for Ti'ek and the other biologists to come in. They crowded around, frantically trying to find something to do.

Sara grabbed Kessler and whispered, "My lung... is... filling..."

Kessler hushed the scientists. He relayed what Sara had told him. They worked quickly and efficiently. Sara moaned as they stuck the needle between her ribs. They pulled out a full vial of fluid. Kessler stood back as the biologists rushed about the room.

He clutched his document.

Hours later, when Sara's condition was stable, he asked one of the biologists what was wrong with her. The biologist tried to find a diplomatic way of saying he didn't know. Kessler sat down next to Sara.

"I should tell you." Her voice was weak. "I'm dying. You know that word?"

Kessler shifted from one foot to the other, his claws clicking on the hard floor. "Odlithian?"

Sara waved at the rows of pods. "All the people, all the humans sleeping in this room, are all dying of the same disease. It's incurable. The disease will affect my brain. Then it will kill me."

"O'aye did not you tell I this dethore?" Kessler grasped at the words.

"Because it was obvious you had never seen a human being until me. We must all be dead."

Kessler said nothing.

"That means that the cure was never found. There's nothing you can do."

"O'ee are scientists," he said.

"Who have only two months' worth of knowledge of human physiology," she said.

"No. O'ee hath nuch knowledge," Kessler said before realizing the implications of his statement. Sara stared at him, her eyes huge.

"Kessler," she said. "Is there something you are not telling me?"

Kessler feigned confusion. "I do not understand."

"What do you know?" Sara grabbed Kessler's fragile arm.

"O'ee learned a lot in the tine o'ith you."

Sara squeezed Kessler's arm and Kessler winced. He was suddenly reminded how much stronger she was than he. She seemed to notice as well, because she loosened her grasp.

"Kessler, tell me," she said, "are there other humans outside this room?"

"No, not like Sara." Kessler chirped.

"What do you mean, not like me?" she said.

Kessler clicked incoherently.

Sara pulled hard on Kessler's arm, using him to lever herself up.

"Not like," he murmured, trying not to fall over.

Once she was sitting up, she took a painful breath. "Show me."

Kessler took a step back.

"Kessler," she said. "Am I your prisoner? Am I trapped here?"

"No. O'ee do not... It is thor thy sathety."

"Then you will not stop me from going up to the surface," she said. She was not asking. She gripped her ribcage as she stood. "I deserve to know."

"I deg you..." Kessler said, "Lie down. Thou o'ill hurt thyselth."

Sara lay back, her breathing heavy, labored.

Kessler's wings fluttered as he held her wrist. "I o'ill take thee in the norning."

Part II

Her stretcher was fitted to lines of cable and lifted up a long vertical shaft. Sara recognized it as the elevator shaft that had led to the hibernation chamber under the ETI facilities. Sara tried to focus on the streaks of light high above, where sunlight was waiting. Her small companion accompanied her on her ascent, clinging to the cable above her, watching her intently. His eyes, in the gloom of the shaft, looked like tiny pools of water. Despite their weeks together, she still could not read his expression. The sclerae of his eyes were dark, unfathomable, like a lizard's—yet it was hard for her to think of Kessler as a lizard. His intellect was impressive, astounding even. And yet he displayed such simple compassion for her. Shakespeare had been an apt primer for his understanding of humanity.

Kessler's colleagues climbed the walls, their skin shimmering, beaks clicking, long tails twitching; they seemed unable to hold still. Yet, despite their unreadable black eyes and greenish scales, they watched her in a way she instinctively recognized. They observed her like scientists, with deep interest, but without judgment. It was familiar, comforting.

She shielded her eyes as she was carried out of the ruins of her research building. The oppressive muggy air wrapped around her. She winced when a grayish alien with a red sash and several medical bags adjusted the tubes running from her chest. This alien had been looking after her medical needs since she awoke. Knowing the disease that infected her, she did not envy him.

As the group crested a hill, Sara saw the landscape of what had once been her city. She recognized none of it. The world of concrete and glass, asphalt and plastic, had been completely swallowed. Everything was green—overwhelming, deep, powerful green. She would never have believed this was Miami if not for the rusted remains of the Carnegie Research Center, jammed into the earth like a broken knife. She tried to locate the remnants of the stadium and the College of Medicine, but they were gone. Miami Beach was nowhere to be seen, swallowed by the sea. She imagined much of Florida was now underwater.

As they bore her through the forest, Sara stared up at the forest canopy. She noticed a large dull orange bulb, wrapped around the thick trunk of a tree. An alien emerged from a hatch in the side and glided through the trees.

Other aliens climbed out of the bulbs to watch the arriving procession. Some of them circled above her. Kessler, always protective, hissed at them, his wings spreading, and they scattered, scrambling up into the canopy.

Kessler led the group to the only structure that was built on the ground. Unlike the bulbs, it was large, spacious, made of wooden planks. Sara's stretcher was gently placed beside it. As an alien with a medical pack examined her, Sara watched Kessler's animated yet hushed conversation with another scientist. Their short, delicate arms hung limply by their sides as they spoke, but their tails whipped about in a frenzy. Sara couldn't pick out any of the words—but it looked as if they were arguing. Finally, Kessler broke off the conversation with a swat of his tail, and approached Sara.

"What's happening?" she asked.

"Thou deserth to know," he said. "Renender, o'ee o'ill not hurt thee. Dost thou understand?"

Sara held onto Kessler's hand as the aliens lifted her stretcher. The doors opened and she finally saw what Kessler had been keeping from her. The building was a barn, filled with stalls. Each stall floor was lined with hay, and each resident was staring at her, dull-eyed, uncomprehending.

"Oh, my God!" Sara struggled to sit up. "They're still alive! Put me down!"

They lowered her stretcher onto the straw.

"Bring one of them here."

Kessler opened a stall gate and guided a girl to her side. Sara touched her round face gently, examining her small almond-shaped eyes, her tiny ears. She put her head to the girl's chest, checked her hands.

"She's showing signs," she murmured to herself. "How old is she?"

Kessler spoke with the grayish alien for a moment.

"Eighteen years," he said.

She checked the girl's nails. "This is remarkable. She has the disease, but it's not killing her," she looked over at Kessler. "Can they speak?"

Kessler shook his head. "No. O'ee are sorry. O'ee did not know."

"Well how could you?" she said, absorbed by this new discovery. "She is showing signs of the later stages of the disease, but for some reason, she isn't dying. Do you see?"

"She hath sickness?"

"Yes. She must possess some genetic mutation that somehow keeps her alive, even after contracting the virus. There is massive cognitive damage, but do you see what this means? It means that there is a way to resist the disease!"

"They all ... hath sickness...?"

"They all have the disease. It's teratogenic. It transfers to the children. That's why they all have it. But they don't die of it!"

Kessler said nothing. Sara noticed the silence that had fallen over the other scientists.

"This is a major breakthrough," she said. "I worked to cure the disease for years. But I never found a single person who survived. Now that I have, I can solve this! And if not, there are dozens of other scientists in those pods who have devoted their lives to..."

The aliens seemed to be shivering. There was something she was not seeing. She looked into Kessler's fathomless black eyes for some sign. Then a horrible thought came to her.

"Why are they in stalls?" she demanded.

"O'ee didn't know... O'hen Ri'ik traveled here. Ri'ik took thood with us. Old o'rld thood. Our thood did not last. Ri'ik landed o'ith no thood. Ri'ik o'er starthing."

Sara covered her ears. She imagined the herds of humans, after the pandemic, with no language, no society. They had probably scavenged for berries, small animals. They had survived here, in Florida, where the winters were mild. And to the aliens they would have seemed just like any other animal.

And then she remembered all the times Kessler had excused himself to eat.

"*Why us?*" Sara frantically looked from one black-eyed lizard to the next.

"It... I do not know this 'ord..." Kessler opened his bag. He took out his notebook and began flipping through it. He opened and closed his beak. Finally, he gave up and pointed at his beak, then made a line down to his stomach.

"Digestion?" she said.

"Digestion," Kessler said. "Thor us to digestion any oth the thood on this 'orld. Hath to eat..."

"I get it. You have an incomplete set of enzymes, but... but why *us*?" Sara was beginning to wheeze. "We are made of the same proteins as every other species on this planet. Why people?"

Kessler shifted from one foot to the other. "Not all. Ri'ik only eat the..." He began chirping and clicking to the other scientists. One of the aliens pointed at his own head and Sara suddenly understood. The muscle tissue was the same, but the brain tissue was not.

"You eat our..." She couldn't finish the sentence. She suddenly noticed Kessler's serrated teeth.

"Kessler," she said very softly. "Can everyone go?"

Kessler hissed at the others, and they quickly shuffled out. He turned and gave Sara one last mournful look before leaving as well.

Alone, Sara looked at the faces of her fellow survivors. They approached her cautiously, like curious puppies. A young boy sank to his knees by Sara's side, and leaned against her. Sara stroked his head, and his shoulders drooped, his eyes closed. She patted him gently as the others slowly congregated around her, gingerly laying themselves at her feet.

* * *

The following morning, a group of aliens came into the barn, checked her vitals, shone lights into her eyes. She repeated Kessler's name until they brought him, along with the gray alien.

"I've been thinking all night, and I believe I have some understanding of the problem we face."

Kessler stood quietly while she spoke. She had never seen him so still.

"I understand that to be able to digest any food on this world you must also eat..." She took a breath. "You must also eat the human brain."

Kessler nodded.

"And I think I know why," she said. "The disease that

killed my people is very similar to Kuru. It's caused by a prion, which is a type of protein. You may not understand any of this but, what I'm saying is that the reason you have to eat … us … is because of the disease. You're actually eating the disease itself. A healthy human brain would not provide you the necessary protein and you would all starve."

Kessler and the other alien fell into a hurried conversation of clicks and hisses.

"I understand that you couldn't have known," she said. "I know how you must feel. To you, we were just beasts."

Kessler drew close, his head bobbing up and down.

The other alien clicked. Kessler translated.

"Can you cure the sickness?"

Sara nodded. "I can."

"O'eee can kee—keet you alithe and in health thor long tine. And you can cure the sickness."

"You would let me do that?" she asked.

Kessler and his colleague clicked for a moment. "Oth course."

"Kessler, if I cure all the humans then what would become of your people? You will starve."

"You could just cure sone oth the hunans." Kessler said. "And o'ee could still hath thood."

But Sara was already shaking her head. "We can't have a world where your people eat mine. We couldn't live with that. You couldn't live with that."

"O'ee hath scientist. So do you," Kessler said. "O'ee could renove the... 'rion."

"The prion cannot survive outside the human brain. There is absolutely no way to remove it." But even as she spoke,

Sara began to formulate theories. Maybe she could grow the prion in another mammal. With enough time, if they woke up the other scientists, maybe she could find a way. But she knew what would happen next. People, her people, would kill every last alien. She could clearly imagine how they would justify the genocide after seeing barns like this one.

It was a dilemma with no solution. The fate of her people was now inextricably bound to the fate of the aliens, and it seemed neither could live while the other existed.

Leaves rustled in the wind. She thought of the world, before she had fallen asleep hundreds of years ago, before humans had made diseases into weapons, weapons so effective that the only survivors could hardly be called human at all.

Before they had made the prion.

The solution settled upon her. It was so much simpler than she could have imagined.

"Kessler. I want you to put me back to sleep."

"O'en shall I o'ake you?"

"Don't wake me," she said. She was shivering and her heart was pounding in her chest, but she had never been so sure of anything in her life. "Don't ever wake any of us."

* * *

The procession back to the hibernation chamber began at dawn the next day; a long line of scientists headed by Sara on her stretcher. They brought her through the woods. She sometimes saw a corner of concrete, a metal shard, rusted and corroded. The last remnants of the human world. When they arrived at the clearing where Sara's people slept below the earth, Kessler crouched by her stretcher.

"It is wrong," he said. "This is your o'erld."

"Not anymore," she said.

"O'at o'ill I do o-ithout thee."

"We're not dead. We're just asleep," she said.

She touched Kessler's cool ablated face then nodded to the other scientists to take her below. They brought her to the room with the other pods and they put her to sleep with her brothers and sisters.

Part III

Kessler sat in the cave before the blue and white door, clutching one of the human documents. The other scientists were on the surface discussing what to do next. He knew they would choose wisely. He looked at the document and fixed his eyes on a single letter. Alone, it meant nothing; he could not even pronounce it. But surrounded by all the other letters on the page, its meaning was so overwhelming that he could not breathe ... he could not breathe.

* * *

This story first appeared in the After Dinner Conversation—February 2022 issue.

Discussion Questions

1. How do you know if an animal is dumb enough to be food? What, if any, test or question would you give it?
2. The doctor shows the newly awakened person a book. The person looks at it and begins to cry. What book did you imagine it was and why? Would any book have made her cry?
3. At what point in the story was the right time to tell the woman she was nearly biologically identical to the animals they ate? *(If ever)*
4. Who has the greater right to live, the sleeping Ancients, or the new residents? What is the best way to decide who rules the planet? Does a species have a natural right to preserve its existence to the detriment of another species?
5. What should happen *(or how long should they wait)* before waking another ancient? *(If at all?)*

* * *

Cicada

Ishan Dylan

* * *

Dr. Kamilah Zhang failed to turn up for her eight o'clock physics lecture on a cold Tuesday morning, leaving her students to grumble about *unprofessional conduct*. One student, a philosophy major, even went so far as to suggest — *unethical*.

By nine o'clock, nobody on the planet was still talking about professionalism.

* * *

In the video, Dr. Zhang sat next to a bookshelf. Behind her was a sixteenth-century poster of the solar system. She wore a lab coat over a dark blouse and a strand of pearls.

"It's done."

She pushed ahead without pausing for the words to land, seemingly unaware of their momentousness. "I don't just mean proof that it's possible. The technology for interstellar travel is complete. It's ours. Today."

* * *

But we couldn't make that the headline, of course. Dr. Zhang hadn't published her calculations. We couldn't risk our credibility. Then again—as multiple coworkers vented to me— Dr. Zhang *was* a credible source. It was frustrating. We were about to get beaten to history by the grocery store tabloid aisle.

After an hour of pitches and one shattered coffee mug, the managing editor settled on my draft: *Prototype for Interstellar Travel Complete, Says Renowned Physicist.*

It was honest. Not too flashy. Journalists aren't supposed to make promises we can't support. Our responsibility is to the truth, not dreams. The public deserves the truth.

* * *

Kids deserve to dream.

"When we go to space, where do you want to visit first?" Jade tugged the sheets to her chin.

I pretended to think. "Let's go to Titan. Surface oceans and fourteen percent gravity. The perfect vacation spot."

That earned me the eye roll I was expecting. "You can't surf on Titan, Dad. They're hydrocarbon lakes, not oceans. It's not dense enough. You'd just sink."

"Oh. Silly me." Outer space was one topic I did not have to feign any ignorance on. "What about you?"

"I can't tell you," her face was deadly serious, "because I'm going to an undiscovered planet. I think I'll name it *Shiva*."

"Wow. You've got this all figured out, haven't you?"

"Maybe not the name. But all the other planets are named after Roman gods, and that's not very fair."

"How about *Ma'at*," I offered, "the goddess of truth and justice."

Jade looked at me pityingly, like I was the child who

needed explaining to. "But I already *have* a backup name," she insisted, "Planet Bobby."

Bobby was her pet hamster's name.

I chuckled and kissed her forehead. "I'm sure you can discover two planets, sunshine."

* * *

"She's got nothing!" my boss roared. "Nada! Zilch!"

"We didn't *say* she had anything," I massaged my temples, "just that she *claimed* to have something. I'll report the leak, okay...?"

I stared at the blank document for long enough that my coffee got cold. Finally, I managed to type a headline. *NASA Leak Proves Interstellar Travel Claims Fraudulent.* I stared at the words until they were just black shapes on a screen. Then I made a correction. *NASA Leak Suggests...*

Next, there was the question of why she did it. Everyone at work had their own theory. It fell to me to copyedit them into something usable. I came across more than one contemporary paraphrase of "female hysteria."

* * *

With Jade at school, the house was empty. I used to walk the dog when I needed to get outside. But Scout was dead. I wandered down the sidewalk without an excuse. That year, it was easy to pick out the newly gentrified streets. I only had to look for which trees weren't crawling with cicadas, trees that hadn't been here seventeen years ago.

I watched the tiny marvels squirm from the mulch. *Beautiful things from the earth as well.* The nymphs emerge with vigor. Only a month to breed, only a month, breed breed breed, they thought. *They don't need to know about the stars.*

* * *

April 13th. It would go down in history as the day when... well, *April 13th* happened. No explanation needed. *July 4th. September 11th. April 13th.*

"It's a fake. It's a hack, or a... photo-chop or something."

"Photoshop."

"Whatever. It's a hoax. Do *not* report on this."

I looked back at my monitor, at the same compressed JPEG that was probably loaded on every screen in the world. Rolling red hills. A landscape that, by appearances, could have been from Earth, but of course, that would be impossible. Visible plainly in the Martian soil, footprints spelled a phrase now overwhelming the servers of Google Translate: *Quod erat demonstrandum.* Translation: *believe me now?*

* * *

The FBI found her on a ranch in Wyoming. No spaceship, no magic gateway. Just her, a woman in a lab coat. A podcaster started a theory that Dr. Zhang somehow used the Mars rover itself to write the message—*She's some kind of genius, isn't she? Like, a hacker genius?* The accusation trended for several hours until the internet collectively realized that rovers don't have feet.

It was a striking front-page photo. A pile of shredded paper and scorched motherboards. During interrogation, reportedly, Dr. Zhang smugly informed the investigators that there was still one type of memory drive their technology could not search.

But not even the constraints of reality can stop a Congressional subpoena. Congress opened an investigation into Dr. Zhang's "destruction of government property" under Title 18, US Code § 1361, and article eight of the Outer Space Treaty.

That's what I had to write. The facts. If you really wanted to know what Kamilah Zhang was on trial for, you just had to check social media. Everyone was arguing the same question.

If she had the technology, why didn't she share it?

People fell into three camps. The first declared the April 13th phenomenon a hoax. The second, that Dr. Zhang was extorting the US Government. The third camp declared everything else, ranging from something about alien body snatchers to the sinister machinations of a particular ex-secretary of state.

There was really no point in theorizing. You could just wait for the Congressional Record to release their transcripts.

* * *

The Senate Subcommittee on Commerce, Justice, Science, and Related Agencies was ready to convene the moment Kamilah Zhang touched down in Washington. Congress even came out of recess for the occasion. Senator Huxley presided.

When it came time for her to speak, Kamilah Zhang leaned almost imperceptibly closer to the microphone. "The data from my laboratory are considered records. I made the decision not to refer them to the Aeronautics and Space Administration."

"So you willfully disregarded your duty," Senator Huxley continued, "your... *sacred* duty, which you swore to uphold—"

"That's where we disagree," Dr. Zhang interrupted. "Oppenheimer fulfilled his duty on paper, but what about his duty to the world? Of course," she said, beginning to lean away from the microphone, "of course, he owed his superiors answers. But he could have drawn out the search. Keep them looking into heavy water, for example... buy time for a peaceful end."

A remarkably optimistic view. But that wasn't what Senator Huxley took issue with.

"Destroying government records is treason."

"Please. Some decorum," Senator Hart spoke up. Blue pantsuit. Third in line for the Democratic nomination. "Look, Dr. Zhang. I understand. Here you are," she emphasized with a squint, "with the power to change history."

"I don't want to be Oppenheimer—"

"—and responsibility can be awfully stressful—"

"—I want to be Frederick Banting."

A pause of confusion turned into real silence as Dr. Zhang drew herself up. "Banting. The man who sold the patent of insulin for one dollar, who ensured that his research would save lives rather than generate profit."

"Then follow his example," Senator Hart insisted, "share your research."

"Insulin today costs $360.25 per month," Dr. Zhang replied. "This economy didn't deserve Banting's trust. It will have to earn mine."

"Dr. Zhang," Senator Huxley interjected, "have you had any affiliation with the Communist Party of China?"

"Mister Senator, I think I've made very clear my position on any such profit-driven entities." Kamilah wouldn't let him goad her into producing any sound bites. "Look. I am willing to disclose some details from my research. They are necessary details to understand my decision."

The room quieted.

"The technology that I have developed can transport

matter anywhere in the universe. Senator Hart, imagine what could be done with that kind of capability..."

"We could have clean energy, better waste management—"

"I agree. We could have benefits for all mankind, which is to say—not profits. But is that what Amazon and Exxon-Mobil will think of, Senator? How will you respond when corporations start hosting off-world fulfillment centers far, far away from US jurisdiction?"

The Congressional Record doesn't include air quotes in its transcripts. You'll have to guess where she put them.

"The federal government exists to regulate private industry, Dr. Zhang," Senator Hart said. "It exists to address these very concerns."

"With all due respect, Senator. The purpose of a machine is what we use it for."

* * *

When the FBI took Dr. Zhang into custody, the editorial board called it an "unprecedented breach of judicial norms." They imprisoned her so that she couldn't give her discovery to any foreign governments. That's what we were saying.

I was assigned to write a piece reminding everyone to be very concerned about precedents. Even if you didn't agree with Dr. Zhang, her civil liberties were our own.

It needed to be said.

I would leave it for someone else to say. I decided to call out of work.

* * *

I was on another walk when I heard something hiss beneath me. A cicada helpless on the concrete, its broken legs waggling in the air.

Normally, I'd squash it. Call it a mercy killing. I stared down at the concrete.

We didn't have to be trapped here. There was someone who could help us. *Someone too busy arguing with millionaires on C-SPAN,* I fumed.

The newsroom and the editorial board hadn't been on speaking terms since the announcement. But it was the only thing I had the energy to write.

OPINION: Kamilah Zhang Thinks Her Politics Are the Center of the Universe. She's Wrong.

* * *

I was expecting my coworkers to be angry. It was only fair. Who knew how many hate messages had been lobbed at them because of what I wrote?

What I wasn't expecting was for my boss to walk in with a buddy-buddy smile plastered across his face. I furrowed my brow.

"*Great* timing. Really had your finger on the pulse for this one."

I didn't understand his sarcasm until he dropped an early draft of today's front page on my desk.

Dr. Kamilah Zhang Dead of Apparent Suicide in Federal Custody.

"Good luck out there, Krish. You'll need it."

* * *

Someone had to drive Jade to school. I tried to ignore the scathing looks. A few days ago, all these PTA parents in their smart watches and yoga pants had silently agreed with me. But that wouldn't show up if you googled their names. Not like my op-ed.

I had it out for her all along. That's what social media thought. Why else had I refused to report on Dr. Zhang between the first announcement and her death?

I started taking my walks late at night when the streets were empty. I slept while Jade was at school. I didn't have to worry about work since quitting, but I still couldn't escape the endless theorizing of my coworkers.

If they couldn't have the technology, nobody could. So they killed her.

No, they're dissecting her brain to figure it out. That's why we haven't seen the body.

I couldn't speculate. Only one question consumed my nightly walks.

Why did she tell us if she knew we couldn't meet her demands?

Guilt gnawed at me. A woman was dead, and I was mourning her research.

* * *

"What's that?" I pointed at the piece of poster board in Jade's hands as she climbed into the backseat of the minivan.

She turned it around. *Galileo* was written in bubble letters across the top.

"Nice! Are you gonna study space someday, like he did...?"

"Maybe," she replied glumly. "Ms. Kleinman said it was too late to change my presentation topic."

"Oh. Okay."

* * *

Once Jade was in bed, I flipped open my laptop.

It was just a school project. But it reminded me of something that I couldn't name. It was on the tip of my tongue.

My fingers hovered over the keyboard. I typed the only thing that ever crossed my mind when it was otherwise blank.

Kamilah Zhang.

42,800,000 results. My cursor hovered over the video thumbnail.

Click.

"It's done," her voice came through the speakers.

Click. Muted.

I didn't want to listen, to fool myself into thinking she was there and talking to me. That would mean I could apologize. I looked at the wall behind her. Something had been strange about the poster. Now I saw what. Earth was at the center, surrounded by concentric gold rings.

Galileo would go down in history for defending heliocentrism until he died, imprisoned for heresy. Religion versus science. The passion of Christ versus the passion for truth. Martyr versus martyr. I stared at the poster behind Dr. Zhang.

It was a message. A time capsule.

Everyone liked to imagine that they would side with Galileo. Especially journalists. After all, our first duty was to truth, even if we don't like where it leads. Or the enemies it leads us to.

* * *

Jade asked if she could stay up past her bedtime to join me on my nightly walk.

"Wait up!" she called out a few meters behind me. She was on her hands and knees, parsing through the wet grass.

"What are you doing?"

"Looking for bugs. New ones. There could be a brand-new kind of bug right here! I read that over eight hundred insect species are discovered every year."

I didn't even think about correcting her. Kids deserve to dream. I nodded along, half-listening.

"Bugs bugs bugs bugs bugs."

I stared at the tree trunks, covered with the translucent, amber carapaces where cicadas had crawled from their exoskeletons.

I stared at the empty husks and frowned. They leave behind their old bodies. They do not hold onto old weight to fly...

We never saw her body.

* * *

This story first appeared in the After Dinner Conversation—August 2023 issue.

Discussion Questions

1. The narrator (*Krish*) says, "Everyone liked to imagine that they would side with Galileo." What does this mean? Why would people side against new science? Why might you side with, or against, Galileo (*or Dr. Zhang*)?

2. What do you think are the ramifications of Dr. Zhang's discovery, assuming it is true? Do you think it would be a net positive, or negative, for humanity?

3. Why do you think Dr. Zhang wanted to prove her discovery to the world only to deny providing it? If you were in her situation, what would you do? Do you think an inventor who withholds world-changing technology deserves civil liberties, or do the needs of the many outweigh one individual's liberties?

4. If you had a world-changing discovery that you wanted to guarantee would get out into the world in the most nonprofit-driven way, how would you do it? Under what, if any, circumstances should a world-changing discovery be driven by profit motives?

5. What do you think happened to Dr. Zhang?

* * *

Author Information

The Mind Reader

John Doble's short stories have appeared in various literary magazines and a collection, *Lefty And Other Stories,* was published by Clemson University. His screenplay, "The AMEN Sisterhood," won the Humanitas New Voices Award. John's plays include *A Serious Person* (Winner, Arts & Letters Prize for Drama, Georgia College); *Coffee House, Greenwich Village* (LaBute New Theater Festival, St. Louis; 59E59 Theatre Off-Broadway, NYC).

Mahabbah

Logan Thrasher Collins is a synthetic biologist, futurist, and author. He is also a graduate student in biomedical engineering at Washington University in St. Louis and is the Chief Technology Officer at Conduit. Logan's sci-fi poetry and science fiction have been published in *Andromeda Spaceways Magazine, Abyss & Apex Magazine, Mithila Review, Silver Blade Magazine, Theme of Absence, The Centropic Oracle,* and elsewhere. His scientific research has been published in *ACS Biochemistry* and in *Biological Cybernetics. logancollinsblog.com*

Mayonnaise

Viggy Parr Hampton, MPH is a health care researcher and consultant. She has published scientific papers, research reports, and expert insights on topics ranging from in vitro meat to hospital facility planning. Whenever she's not in her cubicle, she's playing with her puppy, Tater Tot, and creating fictional worlds to take herself and her readers along on adventures.

Bugs In the Valley

Saba Waheed's work has appeared in *Water~Stone Review* (Fiction Prize winner), *The Southeast Review* (Pushcart-nominated), *Bellingham Review, Lunch Ticket, Cosmonauts Avenue, Big Echo,* and others. She was a Caldera 2020 Artist-in-Residence. She co-produces the podcast *Re:Work*, winner of a Gracie by the Alliance for Women in Media. Saba works as the research director at the UCLA Labor Center using research as a tool to elevate community stories. X (Twitter) *@sabawaa*

Sow

Joseph Bodie is a writer living and working in San Francisco, where he received his Master's in Writing from the University of San Francisco. His work has been published in such journals as *The Tishman Review, Newfound,* and *SLAB*. He is currently working on a collection of experimental short stories.

Two-Percenters

CJ Erick stumbled into Dallas in search of love, great sushi, and access to big box stores. Having found all three, he now inhabits the city with his wife and their two ponderous and entertaining black-and-tan hounds. When exhausted from the reckless adventure of engineering, he pens tales of the space frontier, gothic horror, the occasional steam-punk mystery, and other unbalanced visions from caffeine-deranged nightmares.

We Don't Do Faux

Gordon Sun is a surgeon and clinical informaticist exploring the interstitial spaces between healthcare and technology. His stories have appeared in *Daily Science Fiction, The Dread Machine, Please See Me, Penumbric Speculative Fiction Magazine, Mad Scientist Journal,* and other publications.

Pandora's Dreams

Peter Beaumont lives in Melbourne, Australia and is an environmental consultant and writer. Peter studied philosophy at university and is constantly fascinated by the practical and theoretical questions involved in the endless moral and ethical dilemmas that humans face.

Words Of the Ancients

T. Lucas Earle is a fiction and TV writer. In his professional life he has been a factory worker, a robot for music videos, a stuntman, and a puppy wrangler. His short stories have been published in *Electric Spec*, *New Myths*, *The Baltimore Review*, and elsewhere. He lives in Los Angeles with a retired racing greyhound.

Cicada

Ishan Dylan is a conservation biologist and fiction writer from the Chesapeake area. His work is forthcoming in *Exposition Review's* 'Lines' issue. X (Twitter) *@IshanDylan*; *www.ishandylan.com*

Additional Information

Reviews

If you enjoyed reading these stories, please consider doing an online review. It's only a few seconds of your time, but it is very important in continuing the series. Good reviews mean higher rankings. Higher rankings mean more sales and a greater ability to release stories.

Print Books

https://www.afterdinnerconversation.com

Purchase our growing collection of print anthologies, "Best of," and themed print book collections. Available from our website, online bookstores, and by order from your local bookstore.

Podcast Discussions/Audiobooks

https://www.afterdinnerconversation.com/podcastlinks

Listen to our podcast discussions and audiobooks of After Dinner Conversation short stories on Apple, Spotify, or wherever podcasts are played. Or, if you prefer, watch the podcasts on our YouTube channel or download the .mp3 file directly from our website.

Patreon

https://www.patreon.com/afterdinnerconversation

Get early access to short stories and ad-free podcasts. New supporters also get a free digital copy of the anthology *After Dinner Conversation– Season One*. Support us on Patreon!

Book Clubs/Classrooms

https://www.afterdinnerconversation.com/book-club-downloads

After Dinner Conversation supports book clubs! Receive free short stories for your book club to read and discuss!

Social

Connect with us on Facebook, YouTube, Instagram, TikTok, Substack, and Twitter.